WINTERSHINE

A BOOK OF MAPS, PICTURES, LAMENTS
CELEBRATIONS, PRAISE

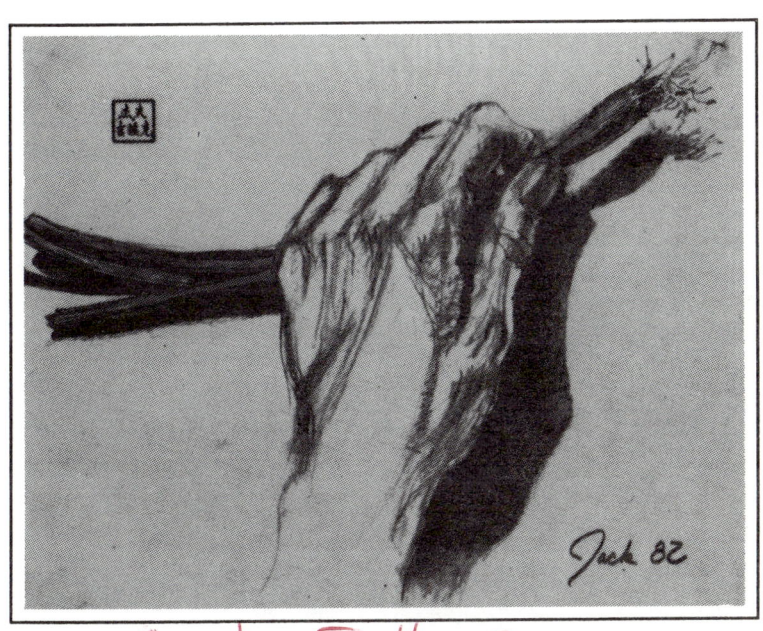

EVE LA SALLE CARAM

ART BY JEFF JACK

Plain View Press
P.O. box 33311
Austin, TX 78764
512-441-2452

ISBN: 0-911051-74-0
Library of Congress Number: 93-086532
Copyright Eve La Salle Caram. All rights reserved.
Art Copyright Jeff Jack, 1982.

Cover art and section graphics are by **Jeff Jack**. The Chinese symbols Jack uses in this series of drawings are his artist's seal. In traditional oriental art, artists authenticated their work by sealing each piece with a "chop," an engraved ideogram of their name.

Also by Eve La Salle Caram
DEAR CORPUS CHRISTI, a novel

With grateful acknowledgment to The Corporation of Yaddo

The author also wishes to thank:
Susan Bright for helpful editing
Megan Bright for proof reading
Marnell Jameson for editorial advice
Ann Dusebout for transcription.

This book was begun in a letter
to William Goyen
and is dedicated
to his memory, and to the memory
of my mother's family.

"I was something that lay under the sun and felt it, like the pumpkins, and I did not want to be anything more. I was entirely happy. Perhaps we feel like that when we die and become part of something entire, whether it is sun and air or goodness and knowledge. At any rate that is happiness; to be dissolved into something complete and great. When it comes to one, it comes as naturally as sleep."

Willa Cather,
My Antonia

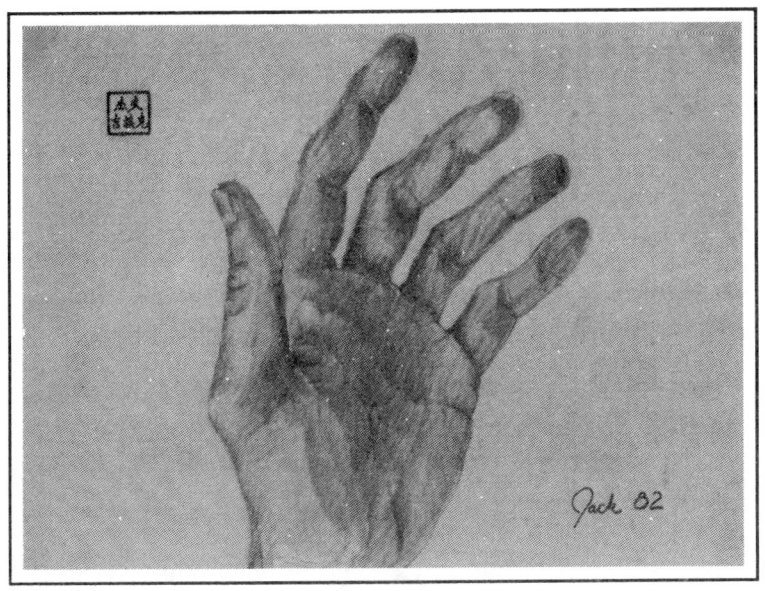

What the Wind Seeks

One day I will detach from the cord that connects me to my mother's voice, to all the voices and all the pictures, even from the steaming green that in summer makes me ache so; and in other seasons from the shimmering ground. "It was a cold spring when you were born," I can hear Lou saying. "I wore a coat to the hospital."

My mother often spoke of danger, of treacherous forces at work in nature; the 1914 cyclone which took her up in a whirlwind and killed the dogs she kept hidden in the basement when it came down, then two decades later the agonies of my birth and of caring for me without a husband or money; and then, after leaving me with grandparents in Arkansas, the hazards of teaching music in the schools of a crude South Texas coastal refinery town, of walking its dusty or muddy streets, and while working in flimsy frame buildings, of braving the hurricanes that often hit the coast.

"Yes, a cold spring." I hear her voice, see her rocking me in a brown wicker chair on the screened in porch of the two-room, tin-roofed shack we called The Little Green House, the Arkansas camp house my grandfather built for Lou after my father went away so she could have a place of her own. Lou wears a heavy sweater which scratches my cheek when I press my face against it. She has wrapped me in blankets on this chilly day in March or April and outside a fierce wind is blowing.

"Yes, like this one, a cold spring. I wore a heavy coat to the hospital. I stayed there ten days, or maybe it was two weeks. I wore the same coat home. Just like this one, it was one of those cold springs that never got any better.

"But I stayed out a lot, had to take the air. They said when I was a girl and had a breakdown that I would have died without the air. Daddy, your grandaddy, took me all the way to New Mexico and kept me out of doors. We made flower boxes."

All her life Louise suffered from bronchial trouble; the attacks began when she was just six or seven, about the same time Daddy bought the piano that she was obliged to practice each day for many hours. Her mother demanded she do it because the piano had cost so much. "Oh, before the light I could hear the boom, boom, boom of the broom handle under my bedroom floor." So it seemed that the first diagnosis might be right, that she was a likely candidate for TB. And yet the doctor the family found in New Mexico, the one all the help had on the Matador Ranch where Daddy worked, said she didn't have TB, only the bronchitis she had always been prone to, said her collapse had been complete because her nerves had broken down.

My mother spoke often of her "nervous breakdown." When I asked her what that meant, she said, "I'll tell you what it means. It means being terrified of dusk, of hating shadows—of dreading the dark and becoming crazy, a little bit crazy when night falls. Since I was a little child I was driven by her—" She meant, of course, her mother. "And by all the family, except your grandaddy, and by myself so hard. In New Mexico the Matador Ranch doctor sent me to a psychiatrist because he said the trouble was in my mind. But, I don't know, I felt possessed, as if something from another realm claimed me, made my brain and yes, my body, its home."

"Don't you feel something coming from a place like that sometimes?"

I did, seemed almost to remember it from babyhood when I looked into streaks of light that reached me from far off, as if from a connecting world.

And I encountered spirits early for my mother spoke of them. When she talked about the house where she grew up, the place the twister hit, she said, "Oh, it was a good old place. Had been a little farm just before your grandaddy bought the property. The man who sold it to him said all his people had died in the house and that it had spirits. And I can confirm that. When I was a girl and couldn't sleep nights—I always did have trouble sleeping—I used to hear them on the stairs. One night when I tip-toed out I saw a little figure—but when I came nearer it was off, a whirlwind off the stair, and then I heard it crying. Like a child. And maybe it was one. Your grandaddy said three or four children were killed in this house in that first storm."

She told me that Aunt O, who was superstitious, always said the whole hill where we all lived was damned. Your grandmother wondered why a smart man like your Uncle Lyman went to Louisiana and got him a superstitious wife. But I wonder if what she said might be true. Sometimes it seems that the earth itself, the very place we are put and call home, and want to care for, is cursed, that demons rise out of the dirt itself and join with others who come from far off, or which are in between ordinary places, and just play hell with us all.

When Louise, whose name means "woman warrior" like a Valkyrie maiden in one of her opera books, when Louise said this to me, I understood for the first time why she starts so many days with a nervous cough. Most of the time that "a caaa-aa-ca-aaa" isn't a real cough but a testing, just a tentative staccato sound. "Young," she told me, "I broke young" as she also said my father did. "I became part of something else."

"God," I asked when I was a child, "please save my mother and father." I was sure my father who had disappeared still needed saving. "And save me from the darkness that would have me, and from whatever it is that passes through—"

My mother's baby brother, Robby, whirls into the spotlight of memory now, Robby the beautiful dark-skinned, dark-eyed young man, the exotic in a light-skinned light-eyed family, remote in my early years, aloof from me until we become years later when I enter school, shy friends. Memory brings me her voice, but blows the sight of him in. When I am three he is just a handsome figure in a white suit in a family and a part of the country where most everyone else wears work clothes—my mother shirts and skirts, my grandmother and Aunt O housedresses; my Uncle Lyman plows the fields or at his work table draws up house plans in his World War I khakis. Remote in first memory from me, Robby doesn't seem interested in, doesn't know what to do around, children. I'm not real to him. I'm not yet real to myself.

Robby blows toward me and then away in the kind of silvery loveliness my mother spoke of when she talked of the theaters she had played in, all the "glamour places," the term she used, with their "pumpkin colored lights."

My Uncle Lyman, the oldest brother and the family seer, opposed the allure of this, just sham, he said. I didn't know what that was, but he warned me against wanting what would finally be nothing, traps set by "big shots" he said, so they could get richer, going to fancy places "like you see at the picture show," dressing up in "picture show clothes."

But I was attracted to the glow I imagined from the lights in my mother's storied theaters and to the shine off Robby's suit.

Memory blows him into the moonlight on the path that leads to The Little Green House where I as a child peer through the porch screen. He walks the path and down the earthen steps that take the family behind it, descends to the bottom of the Green House hill to speak with my mother who is also in white. I open the door to watch them sit at the wooden table which has a summer oilcloth on it and drink from a bottle Robby brings. One day, like my mother's older brothers, he will be poisoned from drinking like this from a bottle. Soon they will leave for town for some sort of party or celebration, significant because there weren't many of those.

Robby moving on the path toward my mother is one of the earliest memories the wind of memory brings me and then whisks away. Another is of my small feet in new brown leather sandals. (When I see Robby I am so shy and he is so bright I always look down.) I love the sight of them and the way they smell as they come down on the grassy earthen steps at the side of the Green House. I like to imagine I follow them, wonder sometimes where they will take me. In later years I got white ones decorated with jewels of clear and colored glass. Always I knew my attention would be divided between looking toward that ground-shine, going with my instincts and deepest needs, and being lured toward a tinsely world of large towns and cities where betrayal would come.

From the beginning I was conflicted, torn between the material and the natural world. But I knew if I asked and really wanted them, I would have helpers to guide me.

One day I will detach from these visions the wind of memory brings and then takes from me, and from the cord that connects me to my mother's voice, to all the pictures and all the voices and from the steaming green that in July makes me ache so, from fuchsia crepe myrtle, from the world and all its blooming things.

She said when she went to see my father in San Antonio, and this was months after he had left us, his mind was so broken that he didn't recognize her when she stepped across the threshold after she opened the door. For me the story she told had the whole meaning of The Depression in it. She said:

"He was sitting in the middle of one of those Persian rugs, peacock blue I think it was with just a little rose and white, one of the rugs his mother gave him and about all he had left to remind him of her after her death. She lost everything in the crash, died in a charity hospital up north. Sitting there in it he gave the thing a center.

"He just looked right through me as if I wasn't there, his eyes almost a watery blue, and I remember them as nearly purple! Handsome as a movie star and with such a sweet smile, always full of good humor. That made almost all the family love him —your grandaddy, Uncle Lyman. But now in this place he had come to, living as he was with the Mexican woman who nursed him he said—she worked as a nurse—he was a pale shell of the person he had been and he sat all slumped over. To tell you the truth I think she kept him doped up; it was easy for her to get drugs.

"The baby is sick," I told him, "and I need money." When I lived in San Antonio with your father I had to steal your formula; I just walked into the drug store and took six packages of Dryco—for that's what your formula was—right off the shelves. And I walked over to the cashier and said, "I have no money to pay for these, but I'm taking them, my baby is sick—I think she may be dying." Then I turned and ran out of the store believing God would forgive me for stealing. I always had good principles—your grandaddy taught me to always have a good principle. I had always been straight with people and still was even when I was stealing their goods. I just explained why I was doing it, why I needed what they had. And then I ran.

"I need money," I said again to your father, "the baby is sick, I don't even have enough for her formula. You know after childbirth which

9

nearly killed me, they thought it best to dry up my breast milk (just after I wished I had it back!) and anyway, they said I didn't have much. But maybe I did! Maybe. I wished they had let me try it. "Yesterday," I told him, "I had to steal it." But still he didn't say anything. He looked emptied out as the room he sat in, nothing in it but a rough Mexican table and a stool or two and that rug he sat on, seemed to grow out of, grew crooked, all bent over, nothing else around him, not even a chair.

Then she came out of a door that must have led to their bedroom. And she shocked me because she was barefoot—I mean it shocked me that a woman would come out like that—and wore only a kimono, so short that it was more like a bed jacket, her black hair loose around her face and in her eyes.

Years later I was surprised when my mother told me this woman who was a nurse gave him morphine to kill his internal pain, that he had a lot, and that without meaning to, he had OD'd.

"He don't talk much," she said, "and he don't want to talk to you. So go."

"I won't," I told her, "until I get some money. I have to have money for the baby."

"He's not working," she said, "and he's crazy now. You have no right to ask for money. You left him for your people, to go back to your people. Get your people to feed your baby."

What she said was true. When he had no job and we were out of money there in San Anton and his mother was dying on charity in Chicago—yes even dying costs money and they had lost everything—well, when he was like that I did go home.

After she died and we had nothing, had sold most of what she left us, all but a rug or two, I did write home to say your father had no job and was acting strange and that you were sick. And I got a telegram that said, "Come home and bring the baby." But it didn't say to bring your daddy. I knew that was your grandmother's doings to leave him out of it. I never forgave her for it.

I went back because I didn't know what else to do. But I thought surely after a while he would write. Would get on his feet and send for me. But he never did. I waited and waited but got no letter. I just sat in this Little Green House rocking you back to life and waiting. But got no letter.

Then one came from San Anton and it told me about the nurse and said that we were through. Your Uncle Lloyd gave me train fare to go down and see what kind of money I could get, but no one in the family ever asked me to bring him back with me if I could do it. Years later your grandaddy apologized to me for that.

"I want his mother's rug," I told the woman. "Rightfully it belongs to our baby. And if we sell it, it will pay for her medicine and the doctor."

"Get out," she said to me.

But your father rose then—oh, he was wobbly but he walked off the carpet and without saying a thing, began to roll it. When he finished, he said, "If Lloyd is with you, tell him he can come by and pick this up." Funny thing was that your Uncle Lloyd was with me.

Uncle Lloyd was my mother's middle brother, the only one who had made any money, was in the wholesale beer business, Schlitz.

"He had driven down in his Packard after I took the train and put me up in the St. Anthony Hotel. I had stayed a night at the Y and he knew I'd be there and that's where he found me. You and I never saw any of it, but he was making money and a lot of it! Though The Depression was on—or maybe because of it—people bought and drank beer.

"I turned to go then, crying, and as I opened the door, a big lump in my throat choking me, my heart pushing against my breast, dried up and empty, the blazing August sun scorching my eyes, making those walls transparent.

"And when I stepped outside and could finally see it, everything and everyone looked so worn out. And has ever since. I figure it's a dying world we've all come into. Since that time I don't think I've seen anything that looked really clean or new."

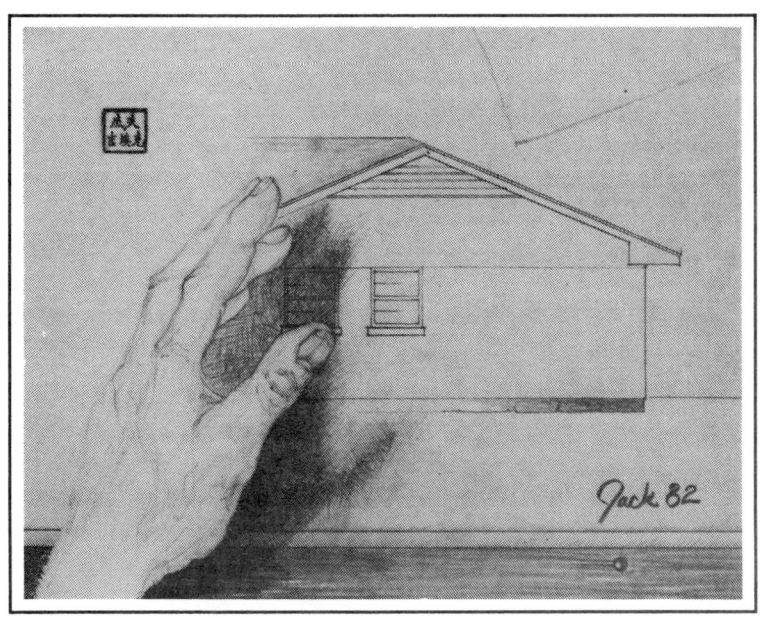

Backfields

When I was young, I just told a friend, the doors to the houses swung open and had no locks.

The world for me just shone!

On the backside of the hill where we lived The Little Green House, rimmed by violet beds and belonging to my mother, glowed with iridescent light.

"A mystery," she said to me many times as we rocked on the screened in porch, "why they want me here, their only girl, in a shack without any plumbing."

So you'll have a place to yourself, I wanted to tell her, so you'll have a place of your own to be alone in or to rock in and talk to your baby.

The Little Green House smelled so good, a good musty smell I loved—that and listening to the rain on the tin roof, a corrugated sheath that protected us from it and became a musical instrument the elements—

sunshine, water, wind—played on; in winter we listened curled up under quilts on the double bed inside and on hot summer nights, lay nearly naked on top of the sheets on the screened in porch listening to the katydids and looking out at the stars. And sometimes in those and other seasons I looked out the back windows at Grandpa's vegetable garden, at the field where it would flower, frosted over in December and in August at the peppers and tomatoes shining and at green beans on poles set exactly the same number of inches apart, looked beyond to the chicken house and to the house where we kept the cow and over to Dread Hill, what we called the slope that rose behind the hollow ("We'll call it that because I dread to go up it," Aunt O said, then asked, "Don't you?"), at the plowed clearing on one side of the woods that led to a corn field where I would play between rows, and to one side of that, to the fence that enclosed two chestnut horses and some cows from Joe Howe's Dairy Farm just the other side of our property.

I still remember how the land slopes, all the valleys, hills and plateaus, still want to name them and greet them. And present them. Give them back to themselves as I also turn them over to you.

The other way—from the top of Dread Hill from the house to the left of the corn field—through thick pine woods, a path covered with pine needles that mostly felt soft to my bare feet, but sometimes pricked them, took me flying to its bottom, to the clear narrow creek with the rocky bottom and the crawdads that I sometimes fished for under them; sometimes I didn't fish but just put my feet in the stream and daydreamed there. Grandpa had made a bench for me, or anybody, to sit on with a wooden box underneath that held a crawdad pole, string looped at the end of it just waiting for bait, a piece of salt pork or bacon. And sometimes he stored hickory nuts in it.

And if he found me there, he sometimes sat down on the bench beside me and told me the story of how he came to Arkansas and about the dreams he had for his children and that they had for themselves. Told me about Lyman, his oldest, who wanted to become an architect, Lloyd the money-maker, my mother the musician and Robby, the baby who when he was only a child sawed the legs off his bed to make it look more "stylish," redecorated the whole house by painting some of the walls bright colors and refinishing or painting furniture, and who had dreams of going out into the world to do more of the same.

Grandpa's mother had died when he was only five years old and when his father who was both a farmer and country doctor remarried, his step mother took him out of the third grade and put him out in their fields to work while sending her own son through all the grades and on to the University of Illinois and then to medical school.

Grandpa taught himself to read and write and figure. He took to carpentry and to building early, knew early he would leave Southern Illinois and strike out for the south and west to a country he could claim that needed bridges and buildings. Made up his mind to build a life there, too.

From sunup to sundown he was out of doors working, spent his summer mornings tending the garden or the corn field, repairing fences and whitewashing the bottoms of hickory trees. He had let Old Pete, the German man I feared, live on it without paying, helped him build a crude hut and encouraged him to work the hillside that ran down to the creek where our bench was. And so Grandpa was accused once by our town cousins of being a German sympathizer. Said to me, "I didn't even know what Pete's homeland was, only that he was far from it, that he couldn't speak our tongue. I didn't know what language that stuff he sputtered was." He had no idea why Pete had come to this country, but said he carried pictures of children in old fashioned clothes who might have been his brothers and sisters and guessed they lived across the sea. But no mail ever came for him and he showed no interest in having his name put on our mail box down on Mill Creek Road or of putting up one of his own. So Grandpa let him be.

The way he let the wildwood be. He wasn't one for cutting trees, only cleared the space he needed at the bottom of Dread Hill before the chicken coop and pig barn to plant a large vegetable garden and at the top of Dread Hill to one side leveled a field that was nearly bare anyway for corn. And he helped Pete clear his hillside for planting. The rest he left, wouldn't have dreamed of selling the pines for timber, hesitated to even cut them for Christmas trees.

"Wildwoods," he said, "protect." He liked the woods for their own sake, and he told me once he believed benevolent spirits lived there. "Remember," he said, "if you are in trouble in the woods and use your sense, they will take care of you."

As he talked I tied a piece of bacon I had in my pocket to the string at the end of my pole and dropped it in the water. "Grandpa," I asked, "do you think I'll get a crawfish?"

"Maybe," he said.

"Or a bigger fish?"

"No, the water's too shallow. You'll have to try at the river on another day."

Small and shallow as the creek was, I knew Pete bathed in it though I had never seen him do it. Once when I saw him at the creek I hid behind a tree thinking I might get to see how he took his bath, but he only bent over to drink some water and then to splash a little on his face. Aunt O, when I told her this, said she had seen him brush his teeth at the creek using a green twig split open at one end. Old Pete's teeth were big and brown and I had speculated he never brushed them.

The hill just the other side of the creek was Pete's to work and live on; he neither owned or rented it, just stayed there, since Grandpa had given permission, and grew several dozen rows of garlic, his main crop and the only one I remember though years later my mother told me he also grew corn, tomatoes and green beans.

Every Saturday evening Pete lumbered down the hill, the garlic in deep buckets tied on either end of a pole he carried across his shoulders. A big old man in I expect almost anybody's judgement, to me he was a giant, in overalls, red beard and mustache, a dirty grey felt hat often crushed down over his huge red head. I was both fascinated and somehow horror-struck by him and, although all my relations said he was kind, ran whenever I saw or smelled him coming.

One day when I was tearing down Dread Hill I hadn't sensed his presence until I was upon him, his overalled hip at my eye level. When I felt the impact of his body, and then it bending over mine—one of his buckets swinging against my shoulder, I wanted the ground to open and take me and believed it might. And yet as he touched me, his rough red face next to my small one, his huge rawboned hands on my shoulders, I still was afraid. Still was even after his lips brushed the top of my head and left his awful breath in my hair.

Then a sputtering of words—I didn't know what they were—came at me. What was he trying so hard to tell me? I didn't know, didn't want to know, not even if it was something wonderful, only wanted to fly out of the place I stood in or to dissolve into it so I would no longer see that big hairy face in front of me, the twinkling grey eyes crinkling at the corners (smiling eyes that didn't fit.) I could hear my own heart beat.

But then it was over. After his hands went over my hair again, as he sputtered on in his ugly tongue (at least to me then it was), he was on his feet and past me, lumbering slowly up the wooded hill, his baskets of garlic swaying side to side.

After he left I forgot the reason I had come in the first place—to dream on my bench over the box with the crawdad poles—and walked deliberately over the stones in the creek and past the rows of garlic on the path that led to the top of "Pete's Hill" and over to the spot where his one room dirt floor house sat and, there, looked in its open door as if to find some answer to the mystery of my own fright. Because Pete was on his way to Grandpa's with his garlic, I knew it was safe to look.

I saw the crude cot he had made from tree limbs and heavy sacking and the black wood stove—like the one in the main room of Aunt O and Uncle Lyman's shack—that he used for heat. A skillet hung on the wall over a nail and on a crate underneath, a wooden plate and a wooden bowl that he had probably carved himself sat waiting. Grandpa said he mostly ate fish he caught and cooked over a campfire, those and wild berries—and maybe squirrel in deep winter—some from the blackberry tangle deep in the thicket far back from our own pine wood near the base of North Mountain, and also wild greens, poke and the like, not considered fit for human consumption by anyone except Aunt O who grew up in Louisiana eating wild things; and persimmons in their season (autumn); and in summer whatever Grandpa gave him from his own beautifully tended and bountiful garden. In winter I had seen my aunt and grandmother give him canned corn and green beans from the shelf. "A man like him don't take to fancy fruit or vegetables," my grandmother said, "so save your pickled beets and peaches, your pretty summer squashes. He wouldn't touch them—why he won't even eat canned tomatoes and with all the potatoes Daddy gives him, they sure would help him make a stew—a wonder he don't have all kinds of diseases."

(Some forty years ago old Pete was found dead on the dirt floor of his house and was estimated by the Garland County Coroner to be approximately one hundred and ten years old.)

The fence just the other side of Pete's crude house marked the boundary of our property. Grandpa had long ago with money from early contracting jobs bought it for next to nothing, or so we would consider it now, more than fifty acres, which wasn't a lot by Arkansas land-buyers standards. Most days if I went at all I moved up the path toward Old Pete's cautiously and preferably with someone: Grandpa, Uncle Lyman or Aunt O, the other "woods people" in the family. Never mind that all of them had told me Pete was harmless and that Aunt O, who had no more idea what he talked about than I did, added he was "pleased at the sight of children" as he had left all those in his family in the Old Country and had no children of his own. I don't know how she knew this. She was inclined to make up stories, her gift to me or one of them. I had given her a new name; the old one was Leola, but when I first learned to speak O was the only letter of that I could say.

As I stood peering into the dark room from an open door I saw nothing that helped me solve the mystery of my dread. But went through it all over when I heard heavy breathing, a kind of easy panting, at my back and then felt something living scratching my shoulders, something cold and soft and living on my neck. Turned to grab the paws and look into the gold-brown eyes yellow spots above them of a shiny black dog, a short hair, but maybe part Spaniel for it had long ears. I only later learned it had Dachshund blood, but was longer legged and bigger and a dog that liked water so maybe it had some Spaniel, too. It licked my face and I hugged it, laughing.

Although I had no idea where this pup could have come from or who it might have belonged to—it seemed a runaway from somewhere—from the moment it licked my face and my fear away, until its banishment (of which I will soon tell you), we were fast friends, and that morning ran away from Old Pete's and down his hill past the rows of garlic, across the tiny creek (it was just a trickle) and up the next hill to the crest at the top, then turned and flew through the gate that took us down Dread Hill (no dread at all to go down) and past the chicken house at the bottom and up the slope past Grandpa's garden and into the Little Green House where after I opened the screen door, I fell onto the bed on the porch and my dark, orange-eyed companion, who became immediately my guardian, jumped after me, rolled with me and sat bolt upright with me when we saw Old Pete with Grandpa out under the oak tree by the wood pile back of Grandpa's Little Spanish House (that was what we had named it) which we could see from the other side of the screen. No more fear! I was home and had a friend with me. And I was glad she had loped over Pete's fence or, more likely, squeezed in through a crack in the gate (that would have been easy for she was so skinny) to find me stealing a look into Pete's cabin and to draw me away from his door. Where had she come from? I wondered. Maggie Fickle's, I thought, maybe, since Maggie was a woman who was known to keep dogs on her little place that sat next to Mill Creek about a quarter of the way into town.

Beyond our boundaries and across the road to the west, we found—after a little oak wood—a clearing and a narrow tributary of some river, in some spots deep, where I was not allowed to go unless grown people were with me. And in almost every summer in my memory the grown people were so hard at work that they went to the river—to wade, swim or fish—on precious few days, sometimes not even on the hottest. But, although I didn't go often, I can still smell the stones and the fast flowing water.

Beyond our boundaries to the north, a red clay road twisted deep into the woods and the Village of Men, Spanish American War veterans who lived alone and in silence, not even speaking to one another, in houses made of felled trees. And although I knew they were peaceful men who would not harm me and who must have mostly stayed in their houses—for I seldom saw one—I was always scared when I walked through their settlement even if Grandpa or Aunt O were with me.

On the path that led to this place and those beyond it, a great blackberry thicket, four or five times the size of the one on our property, grew. And grew. Every year we made our way through more tangle. On the other side, a path no wider than what Grandpa termed "a snake path" led up North mountain to the pumice mine. On this path my grandfather, Uncle Lyman and I, and sometimes Aunt O, found rocks with gold or glittering turquoise streaks running through them as well as the quartz crystals the country was famous for. We filled our pockets and brought them home to bank around trees and porches or to line the bank and sides of our neighbor's, the Appleys', fishpond, which had been Grandpa's creation. Their house had belonged to him before he sold it for retirement, the one he brought up his children in and that my mother claimed was haunted. The one that went up, then came down in the "whirlwind" my mother spoke of so often, the cyclone of 1914 where a winged shape nearly got her on the stair. I'll tell you more about the Appley family who bought it from Grandpa before I'm through. The presence of jeweled stones in the earth and our finding them there always seemed to me miraculous. And of course, was.

All this territory I tell you of lay just beyond the Little Green House which I loved not only because of the intimate way it connected me to Louise, my mother, whose power and sorrow I felt as my own, but also for the mysterious back side of the world it opened onto and that I yearned to penetrate completely. Of course I never did—who could?—and when I returned as a grown woman, found that country cut up by super highways and those woods, almost the whole world for me then, gone. When I was a young child it was both a world I belonged to and God's heart.

"Sometimes it just seems that all the family likes to come down here to humiliate me," Louise said as she rocked in the chair and I lay on the porch bed with my new long eared friend, Maggie. Yes, I called her after the keeper I imagined she had run away from.

"I will never forget the day," Louise went on, "your high felutin' Aunt Jewel walked in on me, all dressed to the teeth in a black fox jacket with great big shoulders over a new wool suit; she had on expensive suede gloves and I-Miller high-heeled shoes and one of those pill box hats, a Gage Brothers, and a good one with a little black veil, pulled to the side of her head, making her more cocky than ever.

"And I was here, rocking like this in a worn out housedress and an old sweater and my scuffed walking shoes, the ones I went hiking with Daddy in. Oh, she liked seeing me here in this little shack without even running water, the big Packard your Uncle Lloyd had bought her parked out on the front of the hill."

"'Why, Louise,'" she said, "'I heard you had not been well and I'm sorry to see you here like this. You look peaked. Is there anything Lloyd and I can do? Maybe you should see our doctor. We'd be glad to take care of the bill.'

"Except for your Grandaddy and your Uncle Lyman, the whole family—Jewel and Lloyd, your grandmother and I imagine even Robby—sometimes he had a chauvinistic side—liked to see me down and out."

"There's nothing the matter with me," I told her, "I feel fine." I knew I looked awful. I wasn't wearing make up and my eyes I knew must have been red and swollen from the crying I had done through most of the night.

"'Well,' said Mrs. Astor, 'I wish you'd let us help you.'"

"It's a wonder I didn't hit her, I wanted to wring her skinny neck. But this was one time I just ignored her, stared right through her and went right on rocking in this chair. So that finally she shrugged and turned and pushed open the torn screen door; this was before I got your grandaddy to mend it—and wobbled in her fancy shoes down the rickety steps. All dressed up like Wallis Simpson and looking like her and thinking she was her (I think she did think that sometimes) or somebody who might well be the Queen of England, skinny pasty-faced thing, cold as ice, Lloyd used to say, cold as diamonds, they sure gave her the right name. If we'd only had Maggie then—she paused to look over at Maggie and me—I would have sicked her on her. Bitch to bitch."

Grandpa built the Little Spanish House, the tiny stucco on the top of the hill, when he was in his seventies after he retired from his contracting business and sold the bigger frame house where he and Grandma had lived most of their lives, on an adjoining property, to the Appleys. Except for the dining porch, the room used by the family the most often, the rooms in the Little Spanish House faced the front side of our hill and a circle of hickories with white washed bottoms which led to a drive marked by squat, spiky palms, large pieces of quartz gleaming in between them with crystals, and the bench Grandpa had built under the big oak at the bottom where daily we sat and waited for the mailman. Past that was Mill Creek Drive, really only a dusty road that wound into town; if we were at the foot of the hill when a car passed, we were all enveloped in a cloud of dust.

The house had two small bedrooms, Grandpa and Grandma's and a plain impersonal "guest room," which was usually unoccupied though once in a while I slept there, the windows of which faced the western mountain. Once when I entered my grandparents' bedroom Grandpa was still asleep and I started to the sight of his exposed genitals, the first male genitals I had ever seen (they looked enormous and frightened me, I thought maybe they had grown on him in the night), for although he wore a sleeping top, he was naked from the waist down. We ate most meals in a narrow, porch-like room at the back of the house and used the tiny, crowded dining room only at Christmas or for rare company on important winter holidays; its French windows faced the front porch as did the living room which held the piano my mother played, a Victrola and velveteen sofa, and on the walls an incongruous mix of gloomy Victorian tapestries in beige and brown that my grandmother had purchased when she was a young bride, and brightly colored serapes from trips Grandpa and Uncle Lyman made to Mexico after they did contracting jobs in Texas.

The front porch, part of it roofed with sloping tile and part exposed, was the most used area of the house and the place where in the evening the family gathered. I used the open part of the porch to try out my roller skates while Grandpa sat reading *The Sentinel Record*, the local paper, from cover to cover every evening after supper and until night fell. But, mostly, the family used the porch just to sit on, to star and moon gaze as they told stories about the past, sing-songy laments or ballads they remembered from childhoods full of troubled adventures, often harrowing or sad. Or stories about their relations, almost always curious or comic tales, or shocking ones about cousins, nieces and nephews who lived in other states or in town, people who had run away from family and taken up with strangers or who had gambled or drank excessively or "lost their minds."

The porch was also, of course, a place of arrivals. Several times a month my Uncle Lloyd and Aunt Jewel came out to the country in their shiny new car with some presents or a load of my grandmother's gossipy, scatter-brained and sometimes small-minded and mean-spirited relations, her niece, child of her dead sister, Hattie, with her teenage girls and young son, who Uncle Lyman claimed was simple minded or her obese bachelor brother, Clarence, so fat the relatives said no woman would ever have him and often an object of ridicule. "Did you hear Clarence at the table last night? Did you hear him ask—after cleaning out every bowl— 'I believe I will have another piece of chicken, Aunt Helen.'" Years later after his death when his sister found and read his diaries, she discovered that the extra poundage had not kept women away. Just after, she marched out to the cemetery and told the keeper that when he cut the graves he should pass Clarence by.

The porch was a place of leave taking and was, after my mother left me there, in my mind, mostly that kind of place.

I was not even three when I stood there in my night shirt clutching a rubber baby doll, unsure of what was happening, why everyone was hugging my mother, holding her so tightly, why she picked me up and held me so tightly, or why she carried such a big suitcase. But somewhere deep inside I knew she would be gone for a long time; it wasn't as if she was just going to spend an overnight with relatives in town. She left with my Uncle Robby who had come up from Texas in his new DeSota to see us. And as they drove down the hill under a full summer moon, she turned time and time again toward the window to blow kisses; her face had been tear streaked when she squeezed me to her, her green eyes glistening, the moonlight highlighting the auburn in her dark hair. She waved and blew kisses when she got in the car, just kept turning to do that. "Bye bye, baby," I could see her saying over and over, her lips pursing to form a hole in the middle—and I thought there was one inside her like that, that she was shot through— "Bye-bye."

I stayed away from The Little Spanish House after that; it had become the house where people left each other. I played mostly outside on the foundation of the house that had once been Aunt O's and Uncle

Lyman's, now a ghost house with ghost rooms. Or I played inside the two-roomed red-shingled shack they built for themselves after their big house burned, just a "camp house" like my mother's they said which had no formal name. All during the winter when my mother was in South Texas teaching piano I stayed with them there (because music students weren't plentiful in Arkansas my mother had to go away) and Maggie stayed, too. Uncle Lyman built a big dog house, one side of which he let me paint with berry stain. He and Aunt O had no children and never would, couldn't have any, though before she married Uncle Lyman, Aunt O had a little boy who was run over and killed by a city bus.

My mother said I made them happy now.

When I was little Uncle Lyman called me "Bea," a name that has to do with happiness, brings it, he said. My real name, the one I had been given, was the family name, "Merrill," though no one called me by it and the role that seemed assigned me was bearer of family sorrow. In calling me "Bea" Uncle Lyman gave me a different designation and set me on another course.

Once he and Aunt O had lived at the top of the hill in the two story frame house that burned down, the ghost house whose foundation I played on. Some say Uncle Lyman set fire to the house himself one time when he was without a job to collect the insurance money, but I never believed that story. Anyhow, he did build the little red shingled house—across the way from, but not quite as far down the hill as The Little Green House, to live in temporarily, just until he got a design or contracting job that really put him on his feet. "Temporarily" turned out to be the rest of his life, not really that long, five or six years from the time I first remember him. I loved to play on the bumpy stone foundation (small colored rocks in the cement), walk around it, look down into the deep grassy pits that held broken tree branches, birds' nests in them sometimes, wild flowers—blackeyed susans in summer—and bramble. If the house were built back, divided into rooms, fine though they might be (and often as I walked or played hop scotch upon the bumpy stones I imagined their grandeur), the invisible place which early had become one of my homes, one of my most important bases, where rooms could change, could shift and glide, would not be.

But the rooms that were there then could shift through each other even as all rooms do in my memory—compartments where some game is played, some challenge met—someone or something confronted—where some drama goes on, or just where some voice is heard, where someone tells a story. In my mind all of us move from one to another (all are finally imprisoning) and in between encounter sometimes, if only in between one or two, something we have come from or yearn to belong to—do belong to, but are separated from, and push on through all the rooms in an effort to get back to—push through those that test us or scare us, those where we merely observe and listen, one or two of which we finally name and maybe learn something from as we move on and on—toward what? The word that comes to mind is "home."

Very young I got some sense of all this when I played on the foundation as sometimes I did for half a day. But as much as I liked in sunlight to turn myself over to this place of air, at night I was always glad to run to Uncle Lyman's and Aunt O's "real rooms" which protected me from all discomfort though the walls that partitioned them from rain and wind were thin. In them I listened to Uncle Lyman read mystery stories by the kerosene lamps or watched his shadow shows on a sheet he tacked up on the pineboard wall (dogs and rabbits and pigs he made with his hands and projected by lamplight) or sometimes heard a record or two on his old crank up Victrola, mostly negro spirituals—he loved he said to hear a good base—although he had one symphony, Dvorak's "From the New World." Or sometimes I just listened to the radio with Aunt O while Uncle Lyman worked over his plans on his card table by the door, slumped over it like a question mark and slight as one (he was so thin!) ruling off spaces, forming beautiful numbers to indicate feet—room size—with newly sharpened pencils. He worked late in total absorption on these plans for houses no one had commissioned him to build and then he'd retire to the big bed where Aunt O slept behind a curtain at the far end of the room. I slept in the feather bed that turned out from the worn cut velveteen (black flowers on yellowy-beige) couch that always looked a little strange in the otherwise plain pineboard room. But because it was properly worn out, it also fit. How delicious when curled up under quilts to listen to rain and wind.

Once or twice a summer, and especially when it rained, Uncle Lyman got up before the light to kill and clean a chicken and in a big black pot start it cooking smothered in home canned tomatoes from shiny glass jars, fresh onions and other vegetables—carrots and potatoes from the garden. Around eight o'clock the aroma of the fricassee which we would eat in the early afternoon would wake me. Uncle Lyman was good at cooking and liked to do it, but mostly I thought of the kitchen as Aunt O's because of the meals she regularly made there. During the day Uncle

Lyman usually sat at his work table in the pantry, a narrow hall-like room off the kitchen, his "office" as he called it, which held an ice box supplied by a mysterious traveling "iceman," whom I seldom actually saw, with large chunks of ice two or three times a week, and a table with his drawing board where he sat for hours working on his plans. Or he was out in the far fields plowing in spring or in summer tending the corn—sometimes when I ran out there to him he let me handle the plow, though I couldn't wield it long and couldn't understand how anybody did.

Aunt O's boiled dinners which she made almost daily in summer—"Let's have a good boiled dinner!"—I liked especially: boiled okra and little round red potatoes with their jackets on and "black-eyed boys" as she called them, the brown pea with the black center (chopped green onion in a dish beside them so we could put it on top) and maybe kale to which she added simmered bacon, and sliced tomatoes just out of the garden and full of flavor, boiled beets and raw onion rings marinated in vinegar and when she could get them from Old Pete who grew them in one of his gardens, little white ears of corn. If she also stirred corn bread up in a skillet, she poured newly churned butter into the broken steaming pieces and put before me at the table where one vegetable was more appealing than the next in its big bowl. Then later she would wrap each bowl in a wet towel and put it in the screened in "cooler" for Uncle Lyman's supper. As often as not, when Uncle Lyman was in the fields, the feast was for just the two of us.

"Aren't we lucky to have all this?" Aunt O asked every day. "Isn't life good?"

Certainly it seemed to me, at least as often as not, that it was. Nevermind that we lived in a poor state in the middle of a great depression that killed my father after taking him away and that broke my mother and caused her finally to leave me and that Aunt O had lost her little boy and couldn't have another and that maybe Uncle Lyman had to burn his own house and had not been able to latch on to a real architecture or building job in months. Deep down a fury burned in me in the place where I grieved (ached with loss). And at the same time our hillside seemed to me glorious, the woods and world beyond mysterious, wonder-filled, the people around me mostly loving, our table overloaded with every good thing the earth could provide, more than plenty unless it was a year of drought and even then enough was canned and put up for us to more than make do. Grandpa used to say, "Why we don't need money." When I was four or five and came to Aunt O's table, and ran over the land and into the creeks and woods and corn fields, it seemed to me we didn't. And when Aunt O and I ate our way into the afternoon and I heard her say, "Why, honey, you've cleaned two plates, I just love a child with an appetite!" In spite of the burning deep inside of me, I didn't know why The Depression, whatever that was, should cause anyone to lose his mind or break a heart.

After we finished our noon meal and covered the leftover food and put it in the cooler and cleaned the table, I washed our plates and the pots, too—I was so proud Aunt O had let me do it (no one else in the family would have let me wash all of these dishes)—as I stood on a wooden crate placed in front of the tin sink where I delighted in dipping my hands, pouring the sudsy water from one glass to another (some were just fruit jars), watching the bubbles run down my small brown arms making the delicate blonde hairs on them shine and looking out the screened window down the slope of the hill and up the rise of the other that began with the garden and chicken houses and ended in woods, while in the other room Aunt O patiently searched for the right piece to fit in her jigsaw puzzle, which she had bought at Kress's—the puzzles piled high next to the scrapbooks and photo albums—when she went to town.

She worked one jigsaw after another, never found the puzzle that stumped her, though some took her months. After she finished she framed them and hung them on the walls—there was Jefferson signing the Constitution, Jesus feeding the multitudes—which everyone in the family except Uncle Lyman said was tacky even in a temporary camp house which they all kept saying it was. After she finished her work on the day's puzzle, sometimes Aunt O napped on the couch with cut velvet figures which pulled out to make a feather bed that was mine at night while she and Uncle Lyman slept in the big bed behind the curtain they pulled that made the space near the back windows a separate room all their own. If after sloshing water back and forth from one glass to another and over the plates and into the pots and over a lot of myself, arms and legs (and the floor), I didn't run right back down the hill and up the dreaded one and into the woods, Maggie along side—and mostly that's what I did every summer day—I would sit at the kitchen table and color Uncle Lyman's cast off plans of houses, office buildings, temples (one of which he finally built for some Baptists who he said weren't worthy of it and would not use well.) Each drawing seemed perfect, even radiant, to me— all those precisely measured squares and oblongs that divided the imag- ined floors, and to indicate their size, all those perfectly executed numbers—perfect circles all those naughts and eights. I could never fathom why he cast off the plans, but as I colored happily, trusted his superior knowledge that the next one would be somehow better.

As I wielded my green and magenta pencils, the man on the calendar picture on the opposite wall sometimes seemed to be looking at me, his face pretty and shiny, more like a girl's face than a man's, no suffering in it—who knew what his body was like, covered as it was in billowing robes? I thought that unless the grown ups had lied to me about what he went through and even had to think about before he went through it, the picture must not be drawn very well and maybe should have been thrown aside. Beneath the firs I knew there were eleven others nearly like it, one for each month of the year. But I liked the colors, greens and purples and gold. And I got caught up in the picture sometimes in a kind of meditation that caused me to drop my pencils and shift my gaze out the big window on the other side of the table to the world outside—to the oak tree and the blue jay who daily sat on the same low branch just the other side of the screen and Grandaddy's stucco house, the only proper house on the hill, just across a wide dirt path from ours behind which the biggest oak on the property grew (mostly we had hickories) where my mother had placed my bassinet when I was a baby and the world and every color in it had first come to me in streaks of iridescent light, the barbed wire fence which marked our boundaries near which Grandpa set his rabbit traps, not too far behind it and on the other side of that, open fields, stretching out toward blue hills, the Ouachitas, a silver tower on top of one of them in the far distance, the lookout for the National Park at the bottom of which lay the town. West of all of it and bathed in what seemed to me surely a celestial light—had all of us come from that?—though I didn't know the word for it then.

The wall that separated me from it and from all outdoors was thin. "We are so lucky to be part of all this," I said one day aloud, altering Aunt O's line by only a little. By what miracle, I wondered, was I?

"What did you say, honey?" Aunt O asked from the other room.

"I didn't say anything, Aunt O." As I said it, I thought her name just right. She encompassed everything, was somehow as complete as a circle.

"I thought I heard you say something."

We are lucky to be part of this, I said, but only to myself this time, joyous, but sad, too. Why sad I wondered? Then I looked again at the face of the pretty falsified Jesus and the calendar of June that would soon have to be turned for it was the 30th and after the passing of that day, when I looked, would be gone and would not come back.

And I knew all at once that the whole world was passing with the afternoon and Aunt O and me with it. And I wanted to stop the world in its passing, wanted to capture and hold it, keep it somehow or at least take the passing to me, shape it again some way and give it back. To whom? I wondered. To you? To myself? To all of us living? But I couldn't I didn't know how. Unless, unless—I looked at the colored pencils I had let go of. Surely they might be good for something other than coloring Uncle Lyman's already nearly perfect plans.

Aunt O's voice came to me from the room with the feather bed, little wood stove and framed jigsaw puzzles on the walls. "I thought I heard you say, We are so lucky to be part of—something."

"Yes," I told her, "that's what I said."

Dear Baby,

I hope you like the sailor dress I am sending and the doll who wears a sailor dress, too. (She had found them both in a town with a lot of sailors, Corpus Christi.) I miss you very much, but I know you are happy there with Grandmother and Grandaddy and well taken care of. I will see you before too long. Until then to my dear little girl, many hugs and kisses.

Much, much love,
Mother

My grandmother read me this letter and many like it over the four years when I lived with her in Arkansas before I joined my mother in Texas and entered school. Those years seemed an eternity—and were, for I have them still.

Lou always signed her letters "Mother" which must have made her feel more like one. She called her own mother "Mother" and was undoubtedly taught to use that address to indicate respect. But when I wrote to her I always began "Dear Mama" which is what I called her and would never have thought to begin any other way.

In part because I wanted to reach my mother so badly I learned to make the letters of the alphabet and use them in words. Before I was three I wrote my first replies to my mother's letters. My grandmother, who won spelling bees when she was a girl before she married Grandpa, spelled for me while frying her popular salmon cakes, with the hot green chili peppers, eggs and crackers in them, on the kitchen's wood stove while I lay sprawled out with my crayons and papers on the cool linoleum dining porch floor. Times when I wrote to my mother were just about the only ones I spent with my grandmother since, mostly I liked to be out of doors, and when I was "in" enjoyed Aunt O's company and her little camp house more.

"How do you make a 'D'? An 'E'?" I wrote lying on my stomach leaning into my letter completely on the green and black linoleum looking up every now and then through the windows' rain spots—for I wrote letters mostly on bad days—"An 'A'? An 'R'?"

Dear Mama
Today it snowed Grandpa nailed a snowman together he nailed two sticks and put snow on them it was skinny the snow slid away I used my crayola to make a red mouth and ears Thank You for the sailor dress Come to see me Love and XXX's

(This letter took me half the day.)
By the time I finished, my mother had lost reality for me as a person or even as a mother and had become a mythical fairy queen who sent presents, fancy dresses and muffs made of real rabbit fur and giant toy rabbits and Easter baskets.
She was also a remembered voice.
And words on a page.

Even after, even during the brief times in adulthood when we lived together—except for the first school years—I thought of Louise as "long distance," thought that most of the time she would probably be away.
"I want to go to the Appleys' when I can," I told Aunt O. "I want Leona to teach me how to draw."
The Appleys lived on the property adjoining ours just across the field in the place where the sun came up. The field began only a few yards past the east side of the foundation and the well where Grandpa had installed a pump for water. All of us, the Appleys and us, lived on one broad hill and, as I have told you, the Appley house had once been my grandparents' house where they raised their children, the very one that took my mother up into the twister of 1914.
Although it was a simple white frame house with an upstairs and a downstairs set behind several big shade trees, I thought this storied place very big and grand and couldn't imagine why Grandaddy had wanted to

sell it to move in something so much smaller that finally, for his children, he and Lyman had to tack up shacks to the back and side. He said he couldn't keep the old place up, that his children were grown though two were still by him, that he didn't do many jobs any more and that he needed something smaller to live out his life in. So he sold the old house to the Appleys who we always thought of as a happy family with two teenage daughters, Geraldine and Leona, and a grown son, Frank, who was away. Leona, the younger and I thought the daintier and prettier one, took commercial art lessons in town where her father ran the magazine concession for the Arlington Hotel. I liked her soft voice, her round brown eyes and shiny brown hair.

On the first golden morning when Leona instructed me, I flew across the path that took me toward her house, the first time all that summer when I was four that I hadn't taken the path to the woods. And I took my first drawing lesson in the old family parlor, the very one which long ago in the cyclone of 1914 had thrown my mother all over it and where, finally, she had hung onto the fireplace grating and later sheltered herself behind a couch from flying glass.

Under Leona's guidance on that day and the days that followed, I drew pictures of girls in green and magenta dresses. (One of the crayolas, a purply red, was called magenta and I was drawn to both the color and the name.) The only other place I had ever tried to draw a picture of a girl was on my grandmother's white stucco bedroom wall as I watched the sun set from the window near the corner of the room. The girl was just a head, round as the sun with hair the color of it and my grandmother switched me for my attempts with the crayolas that shaped a head to set her wall on fire. That's what she said she thought I was trying to do. And as I reflect on it now I think she was right and the fire I made on her wall had blazed from one deep inside me. The girls I drew after Leona's instruction all had bodies and arms and legs, and even feet enclosed in round brown shoes. But I noticed as I finished them that they stood nowhere. I had not drawn ground beneath their feet. And so I used a black pencil to form circles all around them. I don't know why exactly—perhaps I'd meant to make hills— but as I got caught up in doing this, the circles grew and grew into a kind of twister and underneath when I got home I wrote—this time asking Uncle Lyman what letters to use—ME. And then, THE WIND.

Every day I went back to the Appleys to make more and better girls (and circles, and sometimes I drew recognizable hills and roads and even grass and flowers) until I became a pest to Leona and her tall, black-haired, snaggle-toothed sister, Geraldine who often sat with us. "Geraldine is what your mama would call 'stately'," my Aunt O often said, though there just seemed too much of her shooting upward to me.

"Come on," Leona said to me one day, "we're going to take you to the top of the house, going to show you something." The house had a finished room in its attic—a place where the family stored old furniture and mementos. Geraldine led me toward it up the crooked steps from the second floor.

"Do you know who lives up there?" Leona asked—she stood behind Geraldine with me—and when I shook my head, no, she said, "Nebuchadnezzar." Then I asked, "Who?"

"Who, whoo, whooo," echoed the towering Geraldine in a scary voice (deep, for her voice just was, but eerie, too.) "Old Neb," she went on, "our ghost who came from somewhere in between the boards and now lives on the third floor."

I remembered the figure my mother had seen on the stair (and then whirl off it) and heard crying and how she had told me when she was a girl she lay awake at night listening to the spirits come down the stairs, "more than one," she had said, "I can tell you."

"Don't take me," I whispered to Leona, "I don't want to go."

But Leona pushed me up still another stair—by this time Geraldine had darted ahead and I lost the rangy sight of her—and when Leona and I were in front of the opening that led to the attic I heard moaning and something rattling. And I tugged on the hem of Leona's lavender dress (I had thought it and her so pretty) and said, "Take me out of here. Please let me go home."

She didn't answer, just looked down at me. More moaning then more rattling. "Oh," I cried, "please, please let me go home."

I was growing dizzy, became dizzier and dizzier as I clutched the hem of Leona's dress and then looked down at and past my sandaled feet. Did I see something whirling? "Oh, please," I cried. "Let me go home!"

And she did.

"We'd better both go," she whispered as she picked me up—I was half the size of her—and held me in her arms and carried me down the stairs. (By this time I was crying.)

I had never been more frightened. And yet when I got back to Aunt O's I couldn't really believe in Old Neb, only half believed in him. I knew in my bones that the fright I had felt was nothing like what my mother had been through long ago when she heard crying on the stairs.

Deep down I knew the truth. Because I had begged Leona to let me draw and color one picture after another, she had let me and the whole morning had flown by and part of the afternoon. From the time I got there I saw she and Geraldine who was in a bathing suit when I arrived, wanted to go swimming at a Thousand Drippings Spring, a great spring with a thousand drippings from inside the mountain in a dark thicket six or seven miles down the road which they could reach only because Geraldine was old enough to drive the family car. I had stayed too long and worn out my welcome. Geraldine had probably made up the story about Old Neb (I was never really sure) and then pretended to be him.

When I thought about it, I knew the moaning I heard from the attic room sounded a lot like Geraldine when she said, "Who whooo, whooo—
"And yet—

The atmosphere on the twisting stairs and the entrance to the attic was so odd and scary. Maybe there was also a real Old Neb. Who was I to say? All I knew was that Leona had wanted to get rid of me. And that made me so sad that when I crawled in Aunt O's feather bed that night I cried myself to sleep. Angry tears. I cried silently but hard so that my insides burned and my throat ached, too.

After that I didn't go back to the Appleys' for a while. "Pumpkin," Aunt O asked the very next day, "Don't you want to run over to Leona's for your drawing lesson this morning?" She had just poured in a little white demitasse cup with a pink rose on it that she had brought from Louisiana what she called "Cafe Au Lait," mostly warm milk with a few tablespoons of coffee in it and at least one big one of sugar.

"No, Aunt O," I said. (I had felt too bad to tell her what happened on the day before.)

And when she asked "Why not?" I answered, "Because I did something bad and Leona and Geraldine don't like me anymore."

"Why, I'm sure they like you just fine. Who could not like you?" She sounded genuinely shocked. "Whatever you did wasn't bad." Then, after considering for a moment, matter-of-factly asked, "What did you do?"

"I wore out my welcome," I said, "like Grandma said I did when I stayed with Blanche and Bruce in town." Blanche was my grandmother's scatter brained, gossipy niece and Bruce her silly son whom I hadn't even wanted to visit; it wasn't my fault that Uncle Lloyd was late in picking me up to take me back out into the country. "I stayed at Leona's too long," I told Aunt O. I didn't tell her anything about Old Neb; it scared me just to think about him.

"Why, that's all right," Aunt O said. "Your wanting to be there with her to learn how to draw such good pictures is a compliment."

"Well," I said, "I'm just going to draw here today."

And so she cleaned off the kitchen table for me and brought me my crayolas. But looked so sad. As if what I had said about my time at Leona's really hurt.

On that day at Aunt O's kitchen table I practiced drawing more girls the way Leona had shown me to draw all the others, and some I gave brown hair and some orange or yellow and on some I colored lavender dresses and on some green or blue. None had any ground beneath her and all were tilted as if a wind blew. And after Aunt O had looked at all of them and admired them, she stuck them in a big manila envelope she found in Uncle Lyman's office and addressed it to my mother. And later in the day put on a hat and pulled a dress over my head (until I was nine years old I sat around in summer with just shorts on) after which she and I drove The Old Bus to town (she let me steer a little), something we had never done before—everyone in the family said she was an awful driver but I don't remember being scared—where we mailed the pictures (Aunt O let me buy the stamps) and ate strawberry ice cream at the Kress's counter. And in Kress's she bought herself a new puzzle and me without even my asking, a rubber baby doll in a sweet rosebud covered jacket and painted on brown eyes and hair. "Now I want you to have this baby," she said, "and to love it a whole lot."

At first I didn't want to take the baby. Dolls were for Christmas.

"Go ahead and hold her," Aunt O said, "while I give the lady my money." She took two dollars out of her purse. "Why she doesn't cost much. She's worth much more. She looks so much like you."

Later as I held my new baby and rocked her, I remembered my mother rocking me in The Little Green House chair telling the story of her life in which so many terrible things had happened and how some had come suddenly—the talkies in 1929 which meant the end of her career playing the organ for silent films in "big city" theaters (Little Rock, Oklahoma City, Chicago) and cut off the income that allowed her to study with the best teachers; and the stock market crash of 1929 which ushered in the Great Depression and took my father's job. And so many storms, beginning with the cyclone of 1914 in which she said the house rose on its foundation and everyone went up in a whirlwind. When it came down she panicked not just for herself, but for her dogs, four strays she kept hidden in the basement. "A little yellow cur," she told me, "and a big red, that's part Spitz and a feisty terrier that had been someone's pet."

"Oh," she said, "there was a wildness in life and terror." And she told me over and over about this storm. Told me so often that I sometimes almost believed my own life began in it.

"I don't remember how the storm started," she said. "Came at once that twister. Out the window I saw the tops fly off trees.

"I heard the sound, like a locomotive, then like screaming right after I crossed the threshold of the parlor where I had come to look for a piece of music I remembered leaving on a table there. I went into that screaming wondering where it was taking us, what it wanted and what I had done to have it claim me. And why we were rising. Oh, we rose fast and then came down hard. And crooked, the wind set the house down crooked. And I haven't felt straight since.

"When that twister slammed us down, the bricks the house sat on tumbled and the crash killed my dogs, just crushed them, flesh, bones, hearts. Until we jacked the house up and set it on bricks again we had to live with the stench of their broken bodies. I like to think they didn't suffer. The big red had such soulful eyes. I couldn't bear to see suffering in them, and the little terrier was so innocent of pain. I played with him a lot, threw balls for him to fetch, at night wrapped him in a blanket from my own bed—he didn't have the thick fur of the others. I filched towels your grandmother never missed from the back of the linen closet for them to sleep on and made up a pallet out of three or four towels rolled together for each big pup. 'Mine, the dogs were mine,' I told her later.

"That look in her eye, I saw it. 'I was all they had except each other. I found them, fed them from the supper scraps. They depended on me to come to them. I held them to keep them from crying.'

"She said, 'I ought to get Daddy's horsewhip to you.' She didn't mean that, it was just her nasty way of speaking, but she knew I feared the whip they used on Bob, the stallion we had who was never really broken. (I rode him bareback, the only one who could.)

"She was the way she was for a reason, brought up hard, the youngest of twelve and talented with a needle—she could make anything—of a hard working farm family. Then when she married Daddy and was only sixteen and travelled across the country with him, her life was hard, too. Though both of them toiled from sunup to sundown—and both were from families that had things—they never could make money. Worked like slaves for what they had and to keep it. Your grandaddy had to all but rebuild the house just after they moved in because it had been wrecked by a tornado even then. He said if it had not been in good shape, well built to begin with, it would have been torn to pieces. Oh, the wind was always out for it and all of us, but even the twister of '14 left it whole.

"If your grandmother wasn't firing up the wood stove to cook, or sewing up drapes and pillow slips, she was making clothes for us and clothes for other people. She had such a gift for sewing that Hubert Mendelson finally let her make copies to sell of the designer clothes he had in his store. Good advertising for him, he said. The ladies would all say, 'Why, Mrs. Merrill must have copied that from Hubert Mendelson's windows.' If she wasn't cutting out material and sewing, (she never did need a pattern), she was mopping or polishing or waxing, and after she was done, wouldn't let any of us in the front rooms, dining room and parlor, unless it was Christmas or our birthdays.

"The cyclone of '14 spared the house, though it twisted it out of shape, and us with it, but that was about all. Took the crops, the barn—killed the cow (for days milk spewed out of its udders) chicken house and all the chickens. Ripped the front porch off. Your grandaddy rebuilt it himself, then in a cornerstone buried his name and the date which he had scrawled on a piece of paper he stuck in a bottle. The storm broke the chimney and all the windows and whisked the parlor furniture that your grandmother spent so much time polishing right out the front door. Tore to pieces and blackened the hand embroidered curtains she had stitched as a bride. Afterwards Daddy rode Barney, our good old horse, to town, bareback and barefoot and dirt-black all over, to tell your grandmother and Robby and the rest of the family in the movie theater about the wind that had nearly taken our place.

"The summer after, Daddy made what repairs he could and we all ran down to the storm cellar after being touched by the slightest gust. Once with Robby I stayed half an afternoon and into the night there. We had our supper from the jars of canned beets and corn and pickled peaches on the shelves. I had been breaking dandelions, making dolls for your uncle when it became all blustery, dolls' hair whisked right from their heads. If only we had been wishing!

"Well, the family had hardly recouped from the cyclone when your grandaddy came down with typhoid and your grandmother had to nurse him all one summer and half a fall. They thought he wasn't going to pull through it. That's when I found out your grandmother cared about your grandaddy, even though maybe he was the wrong one for her to marry. She never showed much in the way of tender emotion. Your grandfather baffled her and that bafflement gave way to rage and helped make her mean. I think she would have been happier married to someone more present in ordinary things, someone she could speak in particular to about the chicken at the dinner table, the one whose neck he had wrung earlier in the day. Your grandaddy you know always got caught up in these big, sweeping plans—to strike out for a new part of the country, bridge rivers in a half dozen counties, build and then come back to Arkansas or build and move on.

"But I found out she did have feeling for him. And she always nursed people well. Even me. Even after I was grown when I was sick I thought everything would be all right if I could just get home to mother.

"Your poor grandaddy! Burned up with fever through all those blistering summer days and, yes, into the fall. She had to boil all the sheets and bathe him with her own hands. Lyman—your Uncle Lyman—helped her carry him to the tub.

"She had all that to go through not long after the cyclone had nearly taken her house and family away. But your grandaddy pulled through. Oh, he was tough as boot leather like all of us, like all the family."

"When I got spots on my lungs and they thought I had T.B., we soon found out that not only my lungs were damaged, that my nerves were gone. And Daddy took me and the whole family west, to the Matador ranch in New Mexico where the men worked out of doors. I slept on an open porch like this one under a heap of blankets, pounds of blankets; it got cold out there in the winter. Sometimes in the early mornings snow blew in across my bed.

"We stayed till I was well—though I don't know that I ever really got well completely, two winters. Times, though, when we got back were harder and harder in Arkansas. Nobody could pay a contractor. Building halted. And your grandaddy and your Uncle Lyman struck out for the Texas coast. That Gypsy streak in both took them. Maybe people who stay in one spot get ahead finally, pass land and accumulations on. Movement, or the urge to it—restlessness—propelled all of us, though I don't know, they kept coming back to this poor place and I ask you, what's it worth? So that urge in them to return, even to worthlessness and danger, that homing instinct, was there, too.

"But, Jesus, God, the family has certainly gotten around, all over this country! Your grandaddy said Texas was the place, that all his children should go and stay there. He and Lyman travelled to parts of it nobody much before had ever been to. Your grandaddy blazed the trail first, then your Uncle Lyman, and finally, they sent for Robby who was just a kid out of high school. He wasn't cut out for the contractor's life, sleeping on the ground, working in the broiling heat all day, sweat just pouring out of him, or in those Gulf coast gales, the wind whipping him nearly to death—bone thin, he was always just a rail—or the winter rain and bitey cold. His lungs, like mine, were never any good; he had bronchitis all the time, even before he started smoking, one chest cold after another. He broke his arms, both of them when he was little and fell from the roof (he had climbed onto it from a tree) and your grandmother made him an indoor boy during the time when his arms were in casts. He would sit by her while she was stirring up cakes; she would drape material around him and feed him angel food batter with a spoon. So they got him a storekeeper's job.

"In Ingleside, Texas, that hole with a refinery, he ran Cage's store and it was a cage, too. We lived in the back and even had bars on our bedroom windows. Cage's Hardware, Furniture and Lumber; it sold everything but groceries. He had a whole room of sofas and chairs which made him happy, for he liked to work with furniture and tell people how to arrange it in their houses.

"Near the front of the store he sectioned off part of the floor space and turned it into a gift shop and ordered music and jewelry boxes and fluted vases in milky-pastel colors, pink and yellow and blue, and real china figurines and he hired a dignified white haired lady who wore linen dresses in those same colors, the mother of a refinery big shot, to show them and they sold real well. Everybody in town came to Cage's to buy birthday and wedding and Christmas gifts. And they all said it was just the best place in the country to do that. But what a God forsaken country! Nothing in it when your grandaddy came but dirt and mesquite near that smelly bay. (I haven't been able to eat shrimp since we lived there.) Nothing decent for people to live in, nowhere for the children to learn, so that finally he and your uncle even built the schools, the very ones I left you to teach piano in. Your grandaddy and Uncle Lyman built the town and a whole lot of South Texas.

"But in the beginning when the first of the building was going on I was still in Chicago playing the pipe organ in the theater to pay for my piano lessons. I made good money, so that I could do that. And I was sure that one day I would be good enough to make a concert stage. But this was before the talkies came in and they were my ruin!"

She met my father near the stage entrance of the mezzanine when she was sitting in a chair between shows daydreaming and shaking her foot and high-heeled silver sandal. The sandal flew off, she said, and hit my father, who was passing by, in the shin.

"When he handed me my shoe he smiled—handsome as a movie star! But then I had my signal to go in. And I thought: I'll never see that man again. Well, he came backstage a few nights later. And he was a gentleman right up until the end.

"After I married him my life was over. The talkies came in, my dreams of a big career all gone. Your father lost his job soon after and we moved in with the family in Arkansas out on the hill. I nearly died in childbirth, rose out of my body and looked down on it on the birthing table—at the legs spread out and strapped in stirrups, like some poor, stricken animal's—while listening to a big organ that seemed to come from behind the ceiling or from some place that was in between things, the ceiling and me or the ceiling and the sky. And oh, I saw the world passing, passing—

"Then you contracted a kidney infection and nearly died. But didn't and I felt lucky until your father lost his job, then left us. Nothing's been any good since. Would you believe that right after your father left, another twister came through Arkansas and at the same time, down where your grandaddy and uncles were, a hurricane struck and tore up the Texas coast? And I wonder sometimes what God wants, why it's like this, what it's all for."

If the world was passing, it would pass *through* me—it *did*, I could feel it, a big wind going through. I wanted to draw as much of it as I could.

Two years after my lessons with Leona it broke my heart when I went to school and a teacher told me I had no talent for drawing. "You have to learn to be neat," she said. "Your color spills over the lines." Though this teacher gave me A's and B's in everything else, she gave me a C in art and a C in handwriting. And once she gave me a C in conduct because I talked too much to my friends.

School was in Ingleside, Texas, then a little refinery town, the one my mother had told me of, sixteen miles from Corpus Christi. In it my mother taught piano, Uncle Robby ran Cage's store, the back of which we also lived in, and my Uncle Lyman, with Grandpa when he came down, built—built houses and banks and stores and, as my mother had mentioned, even the school she taught in.

Before I left Arkansas to go to school in Texas I tried to draw everything I could see out Aunt O's kitchen window, both oak trees and the blue jay who sat in the one in front of me, my grandparent's house and part of the Little Green House, the lookout tower on the mountain in the distance. I tried to get a likeness of some of the things that were in the kitchen, too: the black iron stove, the bowls of vegetables in the cooler, the tin sink where I loved to wash the dishes. But nothing seemed to come out at all the way I saw it and I grew disgusted with myself and sometimes would tell my new baby whom I kept next to me. I rocked her a lot, sang to her early in the morning and late at night. But in between what I did mostly, if I wasn't outdoors, was draw.

I tried not to think about the way I had brought shame to myself at Leona's. But after a long time had gone by, after summer was beginning to be over, I began to think about maybe going back to see her. I would show her my baby whom I had named Rosie after the flowers on her jacket. I would let her see Maggie, too. Always before when I had gone for my lessons I had chained Maggie to her dog house so she wouldn't follow along.

I wanted to learn how to draw Maggie and Rosie and other creatures and growing things: our cow whom I was just learning to milk (though I didn't like to do that much: I wasn't good at it, couldn't get much out), the corn field, and beyond it, our neighbor, Joe Howe's horses. And Uncle Lyman's bantam rooster. He always said it was mine, that he had given it to me. But I didn't want a chicken for a pet. Still, from a distance I admired it—its shiny black feathers with green streaks, watermelon red comb, its sure walk. Once I brought it into the house with me and let it strut around Aunt O's kitchen on the evening that Aunt O had filled a shiny tin tub with boiling water just off the stove for my bath (I would bathe in the water after it cooled down). The steam from the tub really scared the rooster who began to peck at the hot tin sides of it and then to caw! I wanted to draw a picture of it doing that!

I would pay Leona a visit and she wouldn't mind, wouldn't remember maybe that once a long time ago I had worn out my welcome. (By the end of summer "a long time ago" seemed just when that was.) I wouldn't do that again; I would tell Leona to watch the clock—I still couldn't tell time—that after an hour had passed I would have to go home.

So it was that after my bath that September evening under a full moon without asking anyone, in a clean play dress—and I wore those sometimes—Rosie clutched to me and Maggie loping after, I ran toward the

39

big house in the distance as fast as my feet would carry me.

And then stopped, went cold. Across the path, glittering in the moonlight, lay a bright, black snake both fat and long with big round eyes that bugged out a little, beautiful in a terrifying way and somehow intimately connected with me—I knew this in a flash though I couldn't have uttered a sound about it and certainly wanted to be separated from it then. And Maggie, though she let out a little yelp, held still, too.

And then the snake slithered, its head into the grass, and went on. As I should have.

But didn't. I turned and ran back the other way, straight into my grandfather's arms. He had been drawing water at the well and he held me tight and rocked me and told me that from what I said he thought I had come upon a bull snake, a non-poisonous serpent who probably wouldn't have harmed me. But he said I should never cross the field to the Appleys at night when even under a full moon it was hard to always stay to the path and to see.

The next day when I went to Leona's, she seemed glad I was there, and she liked Maggie whom I brought along, brought right in the house and let jump into a curl up in a cane chair next to the table in front of the fireplace where we sat and drew. But when Leona told me to begin whatever I liked working from a circle on a piece of paper, it was not an image of Maggie that I drew but one of a long, fat black snake with bulging black eyes. I thought it looked a lot like the one I had seen and Leona said it was very good, that she had never been so pleased with one of my drawings. Then she showed me how to arrange circles and oblong shapes so that I might try a picture of Maggie. And I did and liked what I made. I used circles for her stomach which because she ate so much—not because she was going to have babies—had grown very large. Maggie thumped her tail all the time I drew this and her round tummy shook.

When I brought the drawings home I wrote Maggie's name under her picture. Aunt O said she would frame it and hang it on the wall above the couch where I slept. But she didn't think we should keep the picture of the snake around. "You drew that very well," she said, "but let's put it in a drawer somewhere now. If we do maybe he and all his kind will just stay down under, too."

And I never did run across him or any others like him again. But one morning when I went out to Uncle Lyman's and Aunt O's chicken yard—a fenced off space to one side of their house—I did see curled up in the first nest around the eggs I thought I'd gather, a long skinny speckled snake, its ugly head raised and hissing at me. After I fled, and I did that quickly, I knew it was a chicken snake, that it was in the hen's nest to eat her eggs (the very ones we wanted for our own breakfast) but that it could also have struck and hurt me. Afterwards in that same hot month (September) when Grandpa took me swimming at a Thousand Drippings Spring, I saw on the far side of the clear pond I entered rust colored moccasins sleeping on a rock on the far bank and I knew the pool was not just mine to use, but theirs, too.

In these times I learned that terror ran right along side beauty in the part of the world I came from, that both unfurled from the place where at the center of creation they were knotted together. I was frightened plenty from the start.

Once when we went berry picking in the big thicket way back in the woods at the base of North mountain (behind the Village of Men), I got separated from Aunt O and was lost among prickly trees and the fat black strong smelling berries for what seemed a long while. I didn't know where I was or what to do and got back to Aunt O only because Old Pete appeared magically from behind a berry bush—I hadn't even known that he had come with us to the thicket—and held out his hand to me, and I took it for, although he scared me, being alone and without direction in a thorny thicket scared me more.

Once when I sat by the well playing jacks Old Pete came upon me suddenly and made an awful face, sticking out his tongue and waving his fingers behind his ears which made me cry and run, though Aunt O said later she expected he had meant to be funny.

Worse than these times, though, were those when I saw and heard the people who were closest to me turn inexplicably upon one another. Drunk on the whiskey that at first was solace to him, Uncle Lyman grew enraged with Uncle Lloyd, who was having trouble in his marriage, the brother who was closest in age but far away in temperament. Sometimes when he drank, he even became furious with Aunt O. Once when she came into the kitchen and saw him drinking a glass of straight whiskey and said "Lyman, throw that away," he raised the rolling pin that had been lying on the counter as if to strike and both of us were afraid.

Everyone said that Uncle Lyman was smart, brilliant even, but that he hadn't had luck and that he took wrong turns. Before he worked as an independent and took on projects that either put him in the hole or on which, after meeting his payroll, he just broke even, he quit jobs or got himself fired—too idealistic and impractical to build what he was told. He quit LSU before he got the all important architecture degree. "I had to quit, Bea," he told me, "I just plain ran out of money and never got any more."

Another time after a hard rain in early April, I stood under the cherry tree at the top of the hill where Grandpa and Uncle Lyman had strung my trapeze and looked out into the evening at the hills that circled ours, then over at the wild roses that grew over the stone foundation of the house my Uncle Lyman may have burned, I heard him snarling at Lloyd. I couldn't catch what he said, but the growling sound the words made was awful. Then I heard Lloyd hurl obscene words back, "fuck" and "fucking bitch," (the first time I ever heard these words were in my family.) I think I heard him say, "Fuck you fucking bitch."

Everyone in the family seemed to think Uncle Lyman had married the wrong woman. Aunt O was lazy they said and loose, had no ambition and didn't care about appearances or if they had things. I had heard Uncle Lloyd say many times that Jewell wouldn't come near him, that she was "like ice, that cold."

Although I didn't know what they meant exactly, I hated these words that made my uncles strangers. But I said aloud, "It's because they are in the middle," what I suddenly knew, that they were in the middle of their lives, had moved far away from the portal, that place of entrance that I was still close to.

I didn't know what their argument was, only felt behind it an animal anger deadlier than the flickering chicken snake's tongue. And I was sorry for them both. But also helpless.

Each was trapped in his own special strain of life (his own brain and body) and unable to lock into any other, let alone all the rest, because he had moved so far away from the source where in some inexplicable way everything, beauty and pain, was tied together in the same central knot. I could see the beauty in the shine on the landscape.

If I felt some terror in it, too, that was because I was afraid of the power I sensed at the source of life; I knew it was one that changed. Even at that moment I felt myself changing, and I suspected that sooner or later changes hurt. Didn't I hurt already for my uncles, for my mother, for my missing father, for all my family?

I wanted to run down the backside of the hill to Uncle Lloyd and Uncle Lyman and point to the roses, the setting sun and to say, "Look how everything shines! Look at the light hitting the mountains," as if my saying those words would save them. But I didn't because deep down I knew my saying the words wouldn't help. They would dismiss me as a child who knew nothing, would say, "Now go on, honey." (My Uncle Lloyd would say that, would say, "Go to your mother, Baby Girl." At best my Uncle Lyman might call me Bea, might say, "Tonight we'll make a shadow show, Bea.") I knew they would have to find their own way out of their entrapment—if that was possible to do.

Then I thought for at least a second or two about the puzzle that I in being born at all got caught in. For I knew I wanted to grow up, even to grow old, to one day be my mother's age and then my uncle's, to travel beyond the hills that on this evening I found, after a hard rain with the evening light on them and set off by wild roses, so beautiful.

It was in me to grow. But some voice that was also in me said: Be careful, take what you have heard as a warning, you too may become enraged in your prison, may lash out, may know little, unless—

Unless you remember. This evening. This moment.

One day when you are in the middle, in the place where they are now, remember and look for routes to help you get out of your skin even while growing in it.

Unlikely as this recall may seem, these realizations, although I couldn't have articulated them, did flash through me in a moment of childhood time that still lives in me, were brought to me through scare, isolation, grief.

Yet mostly during the time of my entrance into the world I felt connected, nearly one with it, even with its most terrible parts. Never more than when I drew at Aunt O's table or lay in the feather bed listening to one of Uncle Lyman's stories or in the dark watching the shadowy shapes of animals and birds he made with his hands—or he and I made together—on a lighted sheet on the wall. Or when I played alone in the woods where I gave names and sexes and histories to the trees and made up stories about their relationships. I would play out the parts and, in a love story, pretending I was another, would kiss the beloved who was, in that place, a tree—or I climbed to the pumice mine at the top of North Mountain with Grandpa or swam with my eyes open under water for a long time in the clear rocky-bottomed creeks, no partition between me and what I saw.

When I went to Texas to enter school my Ozark foothill childhood, except for a summer or two when it wasn't the same, ended and my South Texas childhood, where I lived with Louise and my Uncle Robby, began along with World War II.

Before I left I lost Maggie who had begun to kill and sometimes eat chickens, just gobble the poor freshly killed things down, feathers and all, or so I was told, (and it didn't seem to matter how much dog food or our own table food we fed her). No wonder her stomach grew so big! Not that I actually saw her do this, but this is what they told me—not just my grandmother who alone I wouldn't have trusted, but my grandfather, too. And one day when I was off at the Appleys' drawing, combining circles and oblongs in a way I hoped would look something like Maggie, second cousins, goofy ones who didn't even keep her, came from town and took Maggie away.

This enraged my Uncle Lyman who hadn't been consulted and who had to tell me.

And he called me "Bea," that name for me which finally the whole family adopted. "Beatrice" he told me is for "one who makes others happy." ("And one," Aunt O always added, "who is happy, too.") "Bea," he said, "I have to tell you how they sent your dog away."

Though I hated his news, there was a firmness and dignity about the new name I liked that wasn't in the names the others used for me, "Baby" or "Pumpkin" or "Sweetie" or "Baby Girl;" never mind that I had been Christened "Merrill Ann." They changed that finally on all official records and even in the Bible to "Beatrice Merrill." Merrill was too formal my mother had always said (but the family had insisted on it) and Ann too common. "And I surely never wanted anyone to call you 'Little Orphan Annie,'" though no matter what the records finally said or how much everyone liked my new name, my Uncle Lloyd sometimes did.

"Bea," my Uncle Lyman said, "they sent your dog away and they never even asked you, never asked me or your Aunt O. Your grandma just told Daddy to do it and then called those feeble minded relations of hers in town and they came out with Blanche and her idiot son, Bruce, to get her." He stopped to unscrew the top of a bottle he had in one hand, took a long drink from it, then went on. "'Why don't you get a tablet and write a letter—I'll dictate it to you." He took another long drink then. 'Attention Cousins.' You could begin like that. 'Send back my dog immediately. You spell immediately, i-m-m-e-'"

I didn't hear him finish. I was out the door and flying, up to the crest of the hill, then down the front side of it through our front gate, then down dusty Mill Creek road, up a grade and then down to the bridge that crossed the creek where when I walked to town with Grandpa I sometimes stopped and waded, until I was on the other side in Maggie

Fickle's yard, standing right in front of Maggie Fickle.

I asked her if she had once had a long-eared dog, a mix of several long short-legged, long-eared kinds, a dog who liked water and who had been gone for a while. (I didn't mention her name.) "Yes," Maggie said, she'd had that kind of pup, but run her off when she saw her kill her chickens. "It didn't seem to matter how much pup food I give her or how much food off my own table," Maggie Fickle said, "she was just a chicken killer. Some dogs are. And sometimes the cutest and friendliest ones, too." She saw I had run off and had been crying. "Honey," she said as we walked toward her old car, "that's nature and that's life, and it's cruel and don't make sense, so just don't think about it none." I told her what had happened to Maggie (still not mentioning her name), then how I had found her by old Pete's and taken her home where she had been my friend and how my Uncle Lyman had built her a dog house and how she stayed there most of the time though I sometimes took her into the woods or over to the neighbors with me and then how my grandmother said she had seen her killing chickens and sent her away. Maggie Fickle took my hand then and said, "You're too little to walk back alone. Now I'm going to take you home and don't you worry. Your grandma is right. The best place for that pup is in town with her people who don't have any chickens."

When I came home to Uncle Lyman's and Aunt O's I cried and cried on the cut velveteen couch, and I felt it was all right to cry there. My grandmother wouldn't tolerate crying, would threaten to spank me for it (and would) and even if she had been present I wouldn't have wanted to cry around my mother, to give her any more sadness than she already had to bear.

When Uncle Lyman, who had been out looking for me, came in, he patted me on the head and then handed me a writing tablet. He had a cup of coffee in his other hand and I could tell he was sobering up. "Bea," he said, "one day soon you and me together have got to write that letter. But come on in the kitchen now for supper." I could smell steaks frying and took comfort in that.

Later that night I grieved for Maggie and found her in my dreams (and for many nights after). In the shadow show Uncle Lyman made before I slept, one of the shapes he made but didn't name soothed me most of all, and also reminded me of something I almost remembered but finally couldn't. I didn't know what it was, only that it had large wings.

Sometime later when I was lying on Uncle Lyman's floor drawing letters of the alphabet on my tablet I once again heard Uncle Lyman say, "Take this letter. 'Dear cousins—Please send back my dog." And lying on my stomach looking out the screen door into the last of the summer, for there wasn't much left of it, I asked, "How do you spell 'please'? How do you spell 'send'?"

I drew to celebrate living in the world, to both give back and capture, but early on writing became a way for me to cope with loss.

PART II
Low Places
(More Wind)

In between coming into the world in the foothills of the Arkansas Ozarks and moving to the south Texas coast was the summer trip I made with my mother and Uncle Lloyd through the "Piney Woods," as they called them, of East Texas, much like our Arkansas woods, except I thought, flatter with even more pine trees and less of other kinds. On the other side of Houston where the pine woods ended and below sea level lowlands began, we took the Hug-the-Coast, a narrow two lane highway that twisted through little towns like Port Lavaca and Rockport. I was five years old, a year too young to live with my mother, not old enough to go to school. The Gulf of Mexico's gigantic moon overhung this initial journey to the place a year later I would call home, a glamour from it that had all of us wishing. "Wish on Texas, honey," I can still hear my Uncle Lloyd saying. "Down here the moon is made of money. Wish for dolls and dresses and pretty things."

What all of us should have wished for was a pretty town to live in. On the low-down landscape that attracted refinery and cotton field workers (cotton fields fanned out from the town) and where the stench of natural gas hung in the air, utility rather than beauty had been uppermost on the builders' minds, including those of my relations. "A hole" my mother called it and by her intonation not the kind that anyone would want to fall into.

The little apartment attached to the rear of Cage's store that my Uncle Robby managed was, for all his efforts, dark and uninviting and there wasn't much to look at outside even if it had offered more windows to look out of. Because of the humidity and the intense heat everything smelled musty and of mildew. On the first night I arrived, an unbroken house cat had messed in the corner of the room with the built-in bed (enclosed by a board of green scallops my Uncle Robby had made, steps leading up to it,) where I slept with my mother and which connected to a big, bleak windowless bath with a linoleum floor. I loved climbing the carpeted steps and crawling over the brightly scalloped board to the mattress and over to the windows where I pulled back the green checkered curtains and looked through the screen and the bars at a big sky over the salt cedars Robby had planted to separate the yard he had made from the crude town.

"Oh, it's so crude," he said, "a disgrace, just shit. One day we're going to leave here and we'll live somewhere glamorous, somewhere exotic, San Francisco maybe, or Hollywood."

In the yard the twisting concrete walk he made and lined with nasturtium, flock and canna beds led to an arbor covered with vine; when I walked towards it or sat in the trapeze that hung from the arbor (just like the one that in Arkansas had hung from the cherry tree), I forgot the cesspool just the other side of the fence lined with salt cedars which kept away the stench, forgot the sagging lot the other side of us with its cesspool and the saloon where cow hands from nearby ranches and refinery workers all swigged beer, forgot the miles of fields planted with cucumbers and cotton all around us, and directly across the way, the rattly cucumber shed.

When I sat in the bed my Uncle Robby had made and looked out the window I named the stars, Robby was always the name of the first star I saw. Then: Lyman, Lloyd, Grandpa, Grandma (for I didn't think of them by first names), Mama, Aunt O. The last star I called Merrill, less for myself than for us all, Merrill, in my mind synonymous with "sorrow" was often literally the last word I had for the day.

In the morning in that same bed I woke to Chopin waltzes, Beethoven sonatas, was literally shaken awake for the bed boards trembled with music my mother played. Why I wondered are we not living in some great city where everyone could hear? Why are we living with Uncle Robby in this ugly town?

Later when I went outside, I swang from the trapeze that Uncle Robby hung under the arbor for me. Or sat up in the middle of the yard in the blazing heat after dragging a bench out from the eaves of the building, made of it an altar to the Sun Queen, brilliant and very large, a Great Fairy Spirit, whom I could see when I spread my fingers in front of my eyes, the colored light, broken and compartmentalized—yellow, then rose, then violet—as I looked toward the sun. One day I told myself the Queen of Light would ride out of the sky and the world would open, turn itself inside out, rumbling out of it, then take us, enfold us. Or I would make up a love story and play out both lovers' parts; when after separation they came together I ran toward the tall salt cedars Uncle Robby had planted and embraced and kissed the briney bark of a salt cedar tree, the taste of salt on my tongue after like that on it when I kissed my mother's cheek on a hot day or after it had been touched by rain.

In this town I played with the first friend I can remember, a white-skinned blue-eyed broad-faced, breathy and good natured little girl (easily and happily excited) named Kathleen O'Hara whose mother was friendly with my family and lived in a small but solid brick house, and there were few of those, near the school. Her father, a boiler maker and people said a "good soul" had been killed in an auto accident, leaving Pauline and Kathleen insurance money which my mother said, at the rate she was going, Pauline would quickly run through. She hired a black maid named Jessie to keep house—was probably the only person with a maid in the whole town—wore expensive hats and dresses from the department stores in Corpus Christi and drove a Packard car. Sometimes she and my Uncle Robby went places in it and people teased him about going out with the "wealthy widow woman" who was older, and heftier than he, and from whom he sometimes borrowed money. He had a girl named Mary Beth before he met Pauline, but she was sickly and moved away and then, or so the story went, she died.

I liked to lie on the living room floor of the brick house and color with Kathleen in new coloring books with good smelling paper. We experimented with blending colors our crayolas made, blue and red to make violet, red and green to make brown, all the while anticipating the tuna sandwiches (crust cut right off the bread), Jessie in her fancy black and white uniform, complete with cap, was making us for lunch. After lunch Jessie let us take bubble baths with the sweet smelling stuff Pauline brought back from shopping trips to fancy stores. And after our baths when I had slipped back into whatever play dress I wore for that day, Jessie dressed Kathleen in a freshly starched white pinafore, a new one for every day, and finger curled her wispy blonde hair.

Kathleen and I got along easily from the start, and had in common an important fact of our existence; neither of us had fathers. One day when we were coloring Kathleen put her crayons aside and sat bolt upright and said in her wistful, throaty voice that before her father was killed and when the road was still clear in front of them, she and her mother had both seen a big, dark shadowy figure sitting on the hood, "very tall, very big," Kathleeen said stretching her arms out, panting between the words a little, "bigger than any car." She said she and her mother both screamed when they saw him, that they didn't see the truck which came from a side road until the very second of the crash which crushed her father into the steering wheel. Goose bumps broke out on both of us as she told this story; our hearts beat hard and both of us shed tears, not the kind that are brought on by mere sadness, but by exposure to something unknown and so rarely experienced in our everyday bodily world—and even that was new to us—that it scares.

At the end of this summer when I also rode the big tricycle sent by my father's family—no return address on the package in which it arrived—and played in the lumber stacks with the truck driver's little boy, I returned to Arkansas and spent another year with Uncle Lyman and Aunt O, this one far north of my grandparent's place near Hot Springs and in the Ozarks proper where Uncle Lyman had, in Fayetville, a year's construction job. I don't remember too much from it, though I think it was mostly happy—picking wild plums off trees in woods near the house we rented; drinking sour limeades with lots of ice but not a drop of sugar in them which Uncle L. made by the gallon jar in the stifling office where he worked and I visited; going to a kindergarten that I liked though I felt it was not really school in that small bright room on the upper floor of a white frame house, a place where I wrote in sand in an elevated table-height sand box and read words in bold block letters off baby books; coating my face and arms with flour for Halloween; playing in a nearby creek and being switched once, but very lightly with a switch of my own choosing, by my Aunt O for not coming when I was called; playing outside after dark in front of the house holding the Easter basket my mother had sent and feeling mysterious but powerful throbbing between my legs—a memory which I seemed to have known always though it was new, liking it, yet also being a little frightened, feeling I must keep it secret—a birthday party when the dark leafy green trees outside our house were drenched in rain and nobody much came, only one or two of the invited twelve children from the Presbyterian Sunday School class Aunt O had sent me to (some years Aunt O when she went to church at all went to the Presbyterian and some to the Catholic as she had done before she met Uncle L in Louisiana) and not minding, in fact, l*iking* the quiet in the room with balloons and streamers, our three plates of layered vanilla, strawberry and chocolate ice cream before us (brick ice cream the paper called it) reading an article in the paper about the party which said that all the children had come caused me to form another party in my mind which in time became as real as the one I had actually been to.

    I wouldn't return to Texas until the fall of that year when I was ready to enter first grade. And now of my introductory summer in Texas which I finally came to think of as my native state, I remember not much more than the moonlit ride down the coast with my uncle telling me to wish on the moon and my arrival in dark and heat to my mother and uncle's apartment at the back of the store which smelled of cat mess (and my Uncle Robby's jokes about it "Did you know we live in a shit-house?" He couldn't have then been more than thirty one or thirty two.), that and my first walk up the steps, first crawl over the green boards into the bed where I looked through the bars on the windows and named the stars. And later of riding my trike and playing with Kathleen.

    But when I moved at six the division of early from middle childhood became intensified, sharpened in memory by the dramatic change in place.

    My mother's music and Robby's gift for decoration and gardening and play made the new world habitable, even interesting. Like an artist, Robby created a world of his own and my mother and I lived almost contentedly in it with him. In the enclosed space behind Cage's store with its vine covered arbor, winding cement walk lined with the most colorful flowers, red and yellow speckled cannas among them, tall salt cedars which separated us from the people my mother called "common" and the homely town, we couldn't often smell the cesspool or see Joe McGee's which looked like a rundown version of a saloon in a cheap western movie or the tin roof and ugly stalls of the cucumber shed across from it or the unpaved streets or the long flat rows of cotton fields or the fat shiny tanks of the oil refinery which glittered hideously in the sun.

From the beginning Robby was for me less of a parental figure than a playmate and helpful friend. He comforted me sometimes, this craggy dark-skinned, dark-haired uncle so much darker than anyone in the family that we could have suspected that he was fathered differently if he had not had Grandpa's face. He said "Don't cry," and "There, now there" as he stood over me when I lay sobbing uncontrollably in a fit of rage — despair and grief (and fear), in the "Princess Bed" (his name for it) after one of my mother's outbursts. She grew furious with me often and inexplicably. Over a drink I had spilled, a piece I had not practiced enough and played badly (my piano lessons came at the end of her long day teaching mostly unmusical children), for something I had said that seemed "not respectful." For no reason that I could really fathom or say, I only knew that my generous, warm, long-distance mother, the fairy queen of my heart and speculation and the very mother who had suffered so when I was younger (who had told me her story), and now suffered differently in ways she couldn't talk about, had become a Fury, someone who in her exhaustion the dark spirits she saw on the stairs of her childhood house finally inhabited. Was that somehow because of me?

"You," she screamed, "You! Yeah cry, yeah scream! I don't know what should be done with you!"

Obliterated, I thought, for without meaning to I had turned my only parent into what I thought of as a black whirlwind, or at the very least without being aware invited a dark spirit to do it, one that Louise had seen and I had maybe stumbled across accidentally on the stair.

"Your mother isn't herself, she's worked to death, it's her nerves," Robby would say.

Then I remembered all of her story, the one she told me when she rocked me in the Little Green House chair. And I knew the terror in it worked on her, went into and through her, and back in again, and finally settled. Took up habitation in her, before it lashed out at and terrified me.

This Fury was to me a separate, a different presence from my mother (had maybe murdered my mother) who was overworked, yes, distressed, yes, but warm, caring.

Later Louise didn't seem to remember the way she was or any anger, though sometimes she didn't talk for a day or two. But I no longer felt I could trust the good mother I loved to stay.

In the mornings after I got up and dressed and put the gas fire on under the toast already set out in the black skillet where Louise had put it before she left to give her first piano lesson, Robby came in from the store to comb my long ash blonde hair and gave me some startling styles—upsweeps and French rolls so popular in the 1940's among the ladies I saw pictured in the fashion magazines, to Scarlett O'Hara curls the likes of which the teachers and the other children at Ingleside grade school had seldom seen. Sometimes even Louise who taught down the hall from my school room and who had come in to say "Good Morning" gasped.

When I was in my second year of school, the third grade—the school for reasons I never completely understood, had skipped me and a number of other children over the second—and had the part of Old Nicomas, Hiawatha's grandmother, in the Thanksgiving play, Robby coated the long looped braids he had made with black shoe polish and stained my face with coffee and lots of my mother's rouge. And when I stepped out of the curtains to say, "By the shore's of Gitchy Goomey, by the shining big sea waters," I heard my mother's deep throated cry. It took many washings for her to get the shoe polish out of my hair.

Later when I was the narrator in the Christmas play—and by this time almost all the shoe polish was washed away—a part I landed because I could read well and even more importantly because my voice carried, he put my hair up in a pompadour and French roll.

I loved being up on stage behind the colored lights, the fat bulbs of pink and red, amber and orange, green and blue, the center of a fairy world which held the whole school's attention, in a floor length crinkly blue taffeta gown trimmed with silver Christmas tinsel. Silver tinsel, too, on the manuscript I read from that was pasted to blue construction paper.

> *And there were in the same country shepherds*
> *abiding in the field, keeping watch over their*
> *flock by night. And lo, the Angel of the Lord*
> *came upon them, and the glory of the Lord shown*
> *round about them; and they were sore afraid.*
> *And the Angel said unto them,*

> *Fear not: for behold, I bring you*
> *good tidings of great joy which shall*
> *be unto all people.*

This was my favorite part of the speech. I had to wear the crisp, sheeny dress over a cast on my right arm, broken in October when I fell off my bike as I was pedaling home from school.

Before the play we sang navy-army songs—I had a strong base voice the kids all made fun of but which I thought my Uncle Lyman would like—"Anchors Away," "When the Cassens Go Rolling Along" as well as "America" and "The Marine's Hymn." How often I was told we could lose the war and all be prisoners of an evil power—yes, even those of us who lived on the South Texas coast, far away or so it seemed, from the centers of the world, the country or even Texas.

All childhoods are strange, but particularly strange it has seemed to me, are childhoods shadowed by World War.

My mother by this time had married a safety engineer at the refinery, but as he was in the war in far away Alaska, I couldn't think of him as a stepfather. By the time I was in the fourth grade—and this was the third year I lived in Texas—the war took away my Uncle Robby who in just two years had become a great and lasting presence in my life though I would not live with him again until I was in my teens.

The store under his management began to carry in addition to appliances and hardware, furnishings and gift items, and some of them fine for a little town on the edge of nowhere ("Oh if the world were round instead of flat," my mother always said, "it would stop right here.") For free rent and very little pay Robby put in ten and twelve hour days. Typical of him to slave for others who made money, to work day and night to help them make more; he could never make a go of his own business, was reckless, wouldn't hire the right people to help. He was working late as usual when the big wind came up and the radio said a hurricane was on its way. We had, my mother said as the workmen began to board up the windows, not much warning, not enough to safely leave town.

The storm arrived at a time in my life when I had begun to keep secrets, the time, I suppose, when most children do. I was eight or so and treasured what seemed mine alone, what those who were connected with my beginnings and who took care of me didn't know about, what, in fact, seemed to separate me from them and from all else living, but what I might, if I chose, share with a friend.

I liked the idea of secrets even more than what I had actually hidden away: crystals I had found in Arkansas but never shown or rocks with gold or turquoise streaks and lots of creatures—turtles, horned toads, tadpoles I kept in boxes—and once butterflies I had captured in a jar—

in the small storehouse in the backyard that Uncle Robby didn't much use and where I had permission to play. My house of secrets sat across from the barbecue pit next to the grape arbor. I had been there with my horned toads and with my turtle whose back I considered painting in a rainbow colors when I heard the wind. At the small window I had seen the sky darken and then heard Louise calling, "Baby, Baby. Come in."

"I want you to run fast to Pagent Lyle's," she told me when I did. Pagent Lyle ran the steak and hamburger shack, just a little frame house the other side of Joe McGee's saloon. "Give him this," she said handing me a ten. The radio says the first hurricane of the season, Annabel, is going to strike."

Though the wind was so strong I had to hold on to the sides of the buildings in order to stand, I thought the storm was exciting and though my heart beat much faster, (Oh, I could hear it!), I couldn't imagine really being badly hurt. Forty years before in Arkansas the wind had sought my mother and her kin with a tornado. In Texas in a different way, a wet one, it wanted to get me and mine. By the time I reached Pagent Lyle's I was drenched in hot rain.

The rain really whipped me as I held on the side of the wall of Craig's meat market which connected to our fence and ran toward the street that was also the highway to Gregory, the first little town we drove through on our way to Corpus Christi. Across the highway, the cucumber sheds, empty and forlorn, rattled in the wind and rain, and when I reached the end of the building, I had nothing to hold onto so I broke into a run, the bill my mother had given me for the hamburgers limp in my hand, soaked through, and in spite of my rain gear, I was soaked, too, the big umbrella I carried turned inside out.

"Now remember," my mother had said, "tell Pagent to make a lot of hamburgers, enough to last the night—at least a dozen—tell him we're having people—and if he can a dozen and a half. Tell him Addie and Minnie and their kids are coming to ride this thing through with us and all I have is a pot of beans on the stove and a slaw in the refrigerator and we want plenty of food in the house. Get a bunch of french fries—whatever he can make up—and a bunch of Fritos, too."

Addie was tubercular and sick a lot. He and Minnie, who took in washing and ironing including some of ours, and their four tow-headed boys, lived in a rickety little shed-like house behind our arbor and directly across from the lumber yard. I knew my mother had invited them to our place because she didn't think their house would stand up through the storm. When she said she wasn't sure we would keep our roof, she looked worried, deep lines from the way she worked her forehead in her brow. Although Uncle Robby whistled and sang as he boarded up our windows, I knew fear gripped him, too. He always played like he wasn't worried. In the way of the very young I was pretty sure we would get through. Those who had nurtured me may not have done it perfectly—how could they with times so hard, and what parents ever do?—but they had given me an elemental trust. Our encounter with Annabel was for me part thrill.

At Joe McGee's I grabbed onto the hitching post where there were no horses—not a soul there this day drinking beer—for the wind was about to knock me over. Then I let go and tore off for the next building, Pagent Lyle's cafe, a little frame house dwarfed under its gigantic hamburger sign.

"Pagent," I said just after I got in the door, "Mama says to fix all the hamburgers for us you can—if you can, she says to fix a dozen and a half—" I stopped, impressed with my own speech and handed over the soppy ten dollar bill, "and we want lots of French fries, whatever you can make, Mama says, and packages of Fritos, too. Addie and Minnie and their kids are coming over to spend the night."

"A dozen and a half?" Pagent asked, tapping the counter and staring out in the rain. "A dozen and a half makes eighteen. Are you sure that's what your Mama said? How many kids has Addie and Minnie got?"

"Four," I told him though I figured he knew how many.

"But, see, each one may eat two. Mama says if this money is not enough to put the rest on her bill."

"Eighteen hamburgers," Pagent said again. He was a short barrel chested man with a broad smile and coal-black hair. "You want to clean me out?"

"Can you make that many?"

"Matter of fact I probably can, barely," he said looking out the rattling plate glass window which I thought was going to break, "but count yourself lucky. With this storm blowing in, you're my last customer of the day."

I didn't know where Pagent lived or if he had a wife or children. I had never thought about him being anywhere but in his little cafe. I wondered if he was not going to board his front window. He was always nice to me, happy and smiling, so I liked him and I loved his pan fried steaks, T-Bones which my mother let me charge to her account once in a while as a special treat, and big thick hamburgers with onion, pickle, lettuce and tomato, mustard and mayonnaise, which he made for thirty five cents. I suddenly wanted Pagent to be ok, but I was too shy to ask if he had a safe house to spend the night in, or to invite him to stay with us in ours at the back of Cage's store. Because I had lived a long time out in the Arkansas country, it was hard for me to speak to people. After he made the hamburgers and french fries which he shook out of the deep fry fat to one side of his grill and wrapped thin white paper around them, he put them in two big double paper sacks and filled another with nickel packages of Fritos—and this took him a while, the wind blowing harder by the second—then handed them to me, with two dollars change, took off his apron and folded it and put it under the counter, grabbed his black raincoat off a nail on the wall around the corner from his grill, then came around and went out with me, propping the CLOSED sign up in his unboarded window. Pagent, I wanted to tell him, you'd better send someone down here quick to board your window. In a few seconds more we were both in his blue car, sheets of rain pounding down on it, mesquite trees across the highway bent over. He U-turned the car out into the highway and drove me the half block to the front of Cage's store, closed for business for the day and I thought maybe forever, where Uncle Robby let me in.

"You had better get on in here," Uncle Robby said as he waved and yelled to Pagent who was in the car. He and Addie had boarded up the big glass front windows and we walked together through the lonely looking aisle, lonely in a way I had never seen them.

Back in the apartment we heard the wind moaning and through the cracks in the boards on the windows I could see the salt cedars that lined our fence all bent over and then Addie and Minnie and their boys, all tow-headed like their mother and husky and squat like her, too—Addie was thin and dark—coming in the back gate. Our lights went out early and we burned candles to see by, though the battery-powered radio still cracked with ominous news of Annabel's early wreckage, power lines down all over the coast, a number of small boats destroyed, "the eye of the storm" out in the Gulf of Mexico less than three hundred miles away and moving toward us.

In my mind I saw a huge living eye, sometimes green, sometimes brown and murky, enclosed in a funnel of terrible rain and moving quickly in the wind toward our sunken coast.

My mother and Robby put the hamburgers and French fries on big platters in the middle of the table and then set it with plates, a package of Fritos on each and alongside little bowls for beans and slaw; it was like a big party made extra special by the howling wind and pitch dark out of doors and inside by candlelight. Robby set the big red candle we had left over from Christmas the year before and were saving for the one coming up, in the middle of the table; he had found it on the bottom of the canned goods shelf along with some red paper napkins.

"If we don't eat these early," my mother said of the hamburgers as she put them on the table and greeted the tow-headed boys, "they'll get cold and soggy." I knew, though, that she counted on there being some left over for later on—that was why she had me order such a lot—and that she would keep these in the oven.

I thought the hamburgers the best I ever tasted, juicy as they were and pungent with yellow mustard. I couldn't understand why Addie and Minnie's boys, who took off the lettuce and tomato, didn't finish theirs. My mother explained later that the family live on red beans, light bread and honey and maybe now and then some canned corn and weren't used to garden vegetables or to meat. "That's why they break out in boils all the time," she told me, "they are just too poor to eat right." All through the war Minnie who could not afford to buy meat on what she and Addie made between them, gave their meat stamps away. They ate big bowls of beans which James Lee, the youngest, said tasted "funny" probably because of the salt pork and hot chili peppers my mother had seasoned them with, and all the corn bread my mother at the last minute made in the big black skillet on the stove. I could tell by the way their eyes got big when they first came in and saw the table they had never been in front of so much to eat at one sitting.

After we finished eating and cleared the table, and the bigger boys and grown ups went into the living room, James Lee and I sat back at it to play a board game called Chinese Checkers I had gotten the year before for Christmas. I was never much for games, but I liked this one because of the design on the board and the color of the marbles—green and rose, gold and blue—that came with it. Each time I got it out I was sure I would find something magical to do with it. At the very least I thought I could make an extraordinary design and at best I believed maybe I would learn some secret from that. I was entering a phase of my life that I have never completely come out of when I regarded the world as a place to be decoded. In playing the game, I thought we might somehow find in it a message, a clue maybe to the mystery of where we had all come from, where we were on our way to and nevermind that the rules to Chinese Checkers said nothing about this. I had always felt I was on my way somewhere, and even before we struck out to Texas.

James Lee had never seen a game like Chinese Checkers, but he didn't seem in awe of it, and I was, slightly. I explained to him how to play and as we sat at the table each making our moves the wind outside blew and blew. "I'm goin to beat you," James Lee said. "I'm goin to move all my marbles over yourn and into the point of that there star."

It didn't matter to me—at least not very much—whether or not James Lee beat me. I was more interested in the way the marbles looked on the board. "Oh," I said, "maybe you will and maybe I won't let you. Or maybe the storm will get us both." I scared myself by saying this. "Oh, listen to the wind, James Lee."

"Goin to tear this here house down," James Lee said matter-of-factly.

"Why don't you children move in the other room and get in the bed with your checkers?" my mother asked when she came through. "That way, James Lee, your mother and daddy can get some rest in here." She pointed to the day bed where my grandmother slept when she visited us, just the other side of the table where we ate. This was the only room we had for and extra bed. "You two," my mother went on, "would be nice and cozy in there. And I'll make a pallet for your brothers on the floor."

"Come on," I said, "you've never seen my bed, James Lee. It's real high up. You have to climb stairs to get into it."

At our feet Ellis, James Lee's big older brother, about 13, but still in a low grade in school, threw dice on the floor with the two middle boys only about a year apart and who at nine and ten looked enough alike to be twins, and Addie, always sickly, had already stretched out on the bed the other side of the table where James and I played our board game and where Louise, Robby and I ate our suppers every night, (my favorite being Spanish rice).

Minnie and Robby were still in the small dark L-shaped living room sitting on the blue cloth couch the other side of my mother's piano, pictures of roses and hollyhocks above it, listening to the portable radio they had put on the coffee table. The same radio that a few months later would bring the news of the bombing of Pearl Harbor and the beginning of World War II. My mother and Robby and I would listen then with the man who was to become an absentee stepfather for me.

After I told James Lee about my bed, he looked at me as if he didn't believe me. "I've never seen no bed with stairs," he said—he pronounced "stairs" like "stars"—skipping over one of my green marbles with a blue one. Although I had never thought him too smart, he was quick to catch onto this game.

"Come on," I said, "I'll show you."

Before we climbed the stairs into the bed we changed into nightclothes, one at a time in the bathroom—I into a summer gown and James Lee into the nightshirt his mother had made him out of a flower sack and had brought along with changes for the other boys in an old suit case.

Though the air was oppressive and the wind sounded fiercely, louder and wilder with each passing minute, the bed was a more wonderful refuge than ever. Because the night was hot, though a fan on the dressing table was blowing on us, we sat on top of the sheets, the Chinese Checker board with our unfinished game on it, between us, though as we turned toward the windows with the bars across them and saw the salt cedars and every other thing growing bent double in the wind, we shook. "All them trees of yourn," James Lee said, "All them trees is goin to break."

"Uh-uh" I told him, "a salt cedar is a sappy thing." (what Robby had told me) "They just bend."

"I'll bet they break."

He grabbed my wrists then and we began to wrestle, upsetting our checker board and sending marbles into the bed's corners like pool balls into Q holes.

"Hey, you children," my mother said, breaking in on us as we tumbled, laughing—by this time I had begun to tickle James Lee, "I thought you wanted to play Chinese Checkers? Straighten up now. Would you like me to bring you a little snack?"

"James Lee says the salt cedars are going to break."

"Never mind them trees," Ellis said from the pallet my mother had set up for him and his brothers on the floor where they were still pitching dice. "the wind's goin to rip this here roof off over our heads!"

"No, it won't," I said.

"We're all going to be all right," my mother said. "Now you children settle down and I'll bring you a little snack and maybe after that you can get some sleep. It's the middle of the night and time for us all to close our eyes."

I thought my mother told the truth when she said we would be all right, but as I looked out through the bars I worried about the creatures I had found and hoped they were ok in their jars and boxes out in the storage house. I hoped that house would stay together. I knew my mother was worried about our very roof, that that's why she was pacing around in her old chenille robe. The radio now as far as I could hear it, was all static. I turned my face from the window and moved a green marble on the board. We had recovered just about all of them from the corners. "Come on, James Lee, it's your turn. You aren't sleepy are you?"

"Naw," he said, but without much spirit.

Even in a hurricane James Lee was not much of a companion. I had more fun with his cousin, Albert, whom I met the year before when he lived in Addie and Minnie's house with his mother and father, Shorty and Gertrude. Albert liked to talk and told wild stories and he also liked to draw pictures on the short, sawed off lumber ends (he drew a picture once for me of his private parts) and to play a toy guitar and to sing. Once he told me he watched his father lying on top of his mother pumping her somehow every night after dinner (I didn't believe that) and then he took me into the lumber stacks way up high and in the back where no one could see us and he lay on top of me and rubbed his whole body against mine and that felt good and though I didn't know what was wrong with it—it brought back all that hot burning ache between my legs I had felt often during the year in Fayetville when I had played outside in the dark—I knew we weren't supposed to do it and for a long time I never told anyone (finally I told my mother) and I certainly had no intention of telling James. I had told him about my tadpoles in the store house and the cute horn toads and even about the jar of butterflies I had let him set free. In those times I kept secrets and secrets; tadpoles and horn toads were of the kind I could share.

"After the storm is over," I told James Lee, "we'll find more tadpoles in puddles of water. We'll have fun naming them and watching them become frogs."

Oh, the world would be full of frogs, I thought. We were talking about frogs and eating Ritz crackers and yellow cheese and drinking Dr. Pepper—I loved Dr. Pepper—which my mother brought on a tray to the bed when I heard Robby say it was past midnight.

"What are you young'uns eating at this time of night?" he asked when he peaked in the room. The grown-ups had some time before had seconds on hamburgers.

"Well," my mother told him, "I thought I'd bring them a snack. They are too excited to sleep. After a while I expect they'll get sleepy." After we finished our snack she brought us cards—we were tired of Chinese checkers, we never made a good design and I was tired of letting James Lee win—and we played Old Maid and then Fish, the radio static screeching on and on, the rain pounding and the wind still howling like a wild pack in the sky and for a long time, though my eyelids were getting heavy, just went on; we could still hear some of the grown-ups talking in the living room. "Maybe it's one by this time," I said to James Lee. "I've never been up this late before." Then I thought I heard the radio say it was two and that Annabel's eye was closing in. "Can you believe that?" I asked. "Two."

"The roof," James Lee said, "is going to come off real soon."

The big boys had stopped shooting dice and lay still with their eyes closed, but I couldn't tell if they were really sleeping. From the far room I could hear Addie's cough growing worse. I guessed either he or Minnie or both of them were by this time lying on Grandma's daybed. My mother was probably on the couch, Robby, who usually slept on the screened in porch (and we had boarded that up), on the floor. The whole place we were in was shaking and rumbling, and Annabel's eye was coming right for us. All the same, I could hardly keep the two of mine open. I sleepily thought again of my horn toads and tadpoles. "I don't think I want to play cards any more," I said. "I feel like I may go to sleep." I thought if I did and we got through this, maybe Robby or my mother would make us all pancakes for breakfast; my mother had just taken our snack tray away. That would be something to look forward to. I was nearly sure we would get through no matter how hard our walls shook or how many times the news announcer on the radio said Annabel's eye was right out in the Gulf and heading for us. From what I could make out the announcer said the eye was moving toward Corpus Christi Bay.

"We're going to be ok," I said to James Lee just at the moment when the worst of the storm found us and I saw with my own eyes from the high bed where James Lee and I sat bolt upright the roof torn from the store house out in the yard across from the barbecue pit and sent flying toward the back lot. And my heart sank for my horn toads and my turtle (I suddenly thought of my turtle and I hadn't thought of him for a long time); the tadpoles I reasoned would be all right. I was glad James Lee had let loose some butterflies I kept in a jar.

Then I heard my mother in the front room screaming.

I'll bet every single building will be torn down," James Lee said matter of factly, "this one next."

"I expect," his brother Ellis echoed, "I expect it will be next."

"Hush," Minnie who was all at once in the room with us said. "Do you young'uns all want a lickin? Why are you not asleep?"

"Mama," James Lee said, "this here storm is going to tear the house right down."

But it didn't. The roof from the store house was, from us anyway, the worst that Annabel took. Annabel ripped part of a wall from Addie and Minnie's and James Lee's place—their beds in their house were soaked—so it was a good thing they stayed with us. The storm hit Corpus Christi, sixteen miles to the southeast of us, probably at about the moment I saw the roof fly off my house of secrets. At any rate, the storm, for us, peaked then and though the wind screamed for hours after and my mother worried aloud about what it might take next, it became no worse. At daybreak Robby reached for the box of Aunt Jemima—by this time I was up and in the kitchen and saw him do it—and began to stir up pancake batter.

By the time we had finished breakfast, even the rain had stopped and I asked permission, which my mother reluctantly gave, to go outside. "Be sure to button your raincoat all the way down and keep it buttoned," she said—and this though we were in a stifling August heat. "And put on your galoshes. And, here, take this umbrella." She handed me one of hers that had been in a rack with music next to the piano. "I guess all of us will have to get out today to see the wreckage—"

"Be careful," she shouted after us as we darted through the house, "stay to the walk and don't go far—and look out for snakes. In a storm like this they all come out, sometimes even crawl up the trees."

Once out the door, James and I headed down Robby's concrete walk, now all but covered with water, that twisted its way out to the arbor and around the barbecue pit across from the roofless storehouse. When I pushed the door open I saw that inside the water was deep, would cover the tops of my galoshes. Had the horned toads drowned? They were nowhere in sight—the lid to their box floated toward the door as did the lid to the emptied butterfly jar. Were they all dead now? And where was my turtle? I had wanted to crayola his back in rainbow colors but that meant nothing to me now. I just wanted to see him living. The world was, surely, one big puddle. How forlorn it looked, how desolate and forsaken. Everything seemed sodden, rotten, smelled bad. All I saw around me was more flattened out than usual and I was afraid to look up, afraid I would see snakes in trees.

Except that it dried out some, all outdoors was like this for months, all through the fall which was a time of clean-up and repair. And pick-up (pick-up, pick-up)—all the broken trees, mesquites and even parts of the squat palms, boards from houses, glass from windows, soppy mattresses and ruined curtains that had been pitched into vacant lots. All of this took weeks and even after it was done, houses and yards looked sad and wanting—houses wanting porches, roofing and eaves, buildings wanting new glass windows, yards wanting planting. Everything went on looking bad, smelling bad. The time after the storm was worse than the storm.

Though I was in third grade, this was only the beginning of my second school year. By the time two more came around so did another major storm, one that my mother and I weathered alone, very scared and clinging to each other in our double bed, in the little one room with kitchen frame duplex. Bertha Oest who had managed the store's gift shop lived on the other side. And I learned after we moved she died one night in her sleep there when her heart just stopped. The refinery was then all but shut down, most men, including Bertha's son, her one relative, away at war. My uncle Robby, stationed in San Diego, had been in the navy for half a year and Mr. Cage had closed his store. The second storm whose name I don't remember (was it Isadora, maybe?) was worse than the first—no fun in it—and, after it, every tree in town was broken, even most of the salt cedars and when Christmas of that year had come and gone, most of the women and children who had been left in the town deserted it, too. Teaching piano was for my mother no longer worthwhile—she just didn't have enough students to make any money. I finished the school year out with my grandparents in Arkansas and she joined my stepfather who had been wounded, promoted to Lt. Colonel and sent to Ft. Devins in Massachusetts to sit out the rest of the fighting. (The knee in which he was shot pained him all his life.) The war was over, and although I didn't realize it then—I was eleven years old—my long childhood which seemed almost to have begun in the great storm of 1914, with my mother's story about that, was all but cut off abruptly in another.

School opened as the world dried out and was a place I liked. And much more than I had the year before when it seemed to me we mostly just made with our long yellow school pencils circles and then letters. I liked all the books I was issued to read from and the stories that our bland young blonde teacher read to us in her dull voice. Heidi I liked especially; during the years I spent in low places I liked to imagine and dream about heights. And I liked the notebook I got to keep in Spanish—during this year Spanish was instituted in the schools only to be removed a year after—with pictures of El Gato and El Perro, and the pages I colored red so I could write "Rojo" and green so I could write "Verde" and my favorite of all the color words, "Azul," which I thought the whole world, whether it had ever seen a Spanish book or not, must know was blue. And I liked singing songs in assembly—until I was nine I kept my deep voice—and riding my bicycle, The Blue Bird (which because I spoke Spanish secretly I named secretly, "Azul"), to the drug store and after school for ice cream sodas and a look across the street at the movie marquee—I spent nearly every Saturday and Sunday afternoon at the show and had a huge collection of movie star pictures I had written the studios in Hollywood for. A year later the movie house burned down with me in it when the fire started and for a whole winter we had to see silent films in the Community House. Although Kathleen had moved away to Corpus Christi, she sometimes visited, and we went to the show together or played a mystery game called "Murder in the Dark" in her house or "Statues" where when we were tapped by the child who was "It" we froze in pretty poses; and I liked my new friends, Mary, also an only child—and I thought pretty—whose mother was a high school teacher, and Joanne, a live wire who wanted to be a dancer—we put on shows in the grape arbor where she flashed her dark brown eyes and danced on top of a table—whose mother was busy with young kids (their fathers were both refinery men) and I liked and admired Consuela, who read better than anyone in our class except me, and who looked regal because of the straight way she held herself and the braids across the top of her head, green and magenta yarn woven through them, which she wore like a crown, but who remained mysterious and apart because she lived in one of the little unpainted wooden houses across from a big field—littered with old tires and tin cans—the Mexican families occupied but no one else visited. That fall during a Victory drive for school we collected the tires and tin and then got a clear view of the sad little houses that no one ever spoke of, chickens scratching in their dirt yards.

 I liked the football rallies on Friday nights, the high school band marching down the streets of the town and I liked especially the twirlers. One of the Hill girls—the Hills were refinery big-shots—Baby, and her older sister, Gloria, had won ribbons in twirling competitions and I liked the night of the games when I ate dirt in front of the people in the stands (I liked to show off)—and the Halloween parade where I was a witch in a tall black hat and long black gown and wore rouge and green eye shadow streaked all over my face—I liked that, especially, because always before I had been something pretty. "Oh you are horrible, Beatrice Merrill," Bertha Oest said when I went in the gift shop to scare her. "Beatrice Merrill" was now what everyone called me. And I liked marching with the other Halloween characters, as if we were all in an important play, down the main street to the high school grounds which were set up for a Carnival and boasted booths where people could throw darts or rubber rings for prizes and tents they could sit under to play dominos or bingo, a booth where for fifty cents the PTA ladies served a Mexican supper and even a booth where one of them was dressed up like a Gypsy and told fortunes. My mother said she didn't tell "real" fortunes; my Uncle Robby had been to someone who told *real* ones and the woman he went to told him he would soon leave us for one of the services, she thought the navy for he would be near water though he would not be in the fighting and would never go across it. And that came true; he was stationed in San Diego were he managed the navy store. After the carnival my friends and I rode our bikes down "Silk Stocking Row," a row of ugly gray frame houses where the refinery officials lived, where we liked to knock on doors and yell "trick or treat." It was the tricks we wanted—treats we could always get—draping porches with toilet paper or tipping over outdoor furniture (it would never have occurred to us to be really destructive or hurtful)—so we liked it when somebody yelled, "Well, I guess you can just trick us!" or when nobody was home.

After Halloween was over we got ready for Christmas. Uncle Robby hired an old German man no one else would have to paint a mural of Santa and his Reindeer on the wall behind the staircase at Cage's store, and we began learning parts for the school play as our mothers or grandmothers started sewing up costumes—since I was the narrator I got a long evening dress—and rehearsed in earnest after the break for Thanksgiving. To escape the ugly town and the back of Cage's store we went to Corpus for Thanksgiving dinner in the Morocco Room, which sounded like a place in one of the movies I'd seen, the main dining room of the biggest hotel and to save on gas which was rationed, returned as we had come, on a Continental bus and rode it back the next day to do Christmas shopping. Under my mother's direction I had made up my own Christmas list the week before. All fall I had saved money out of the allowance she gave me. I would give a present to everyone in my family and buy most of them at a department store called Lichensteins: a broach for my grandmother to wear on the new dress she made for church—she went to the Methodist in Hot Springs (was the only real churchgoer in our family) and I was Christened there; a pipe for my grandfather so he could puff to his heart's content while listening to the radio or reading the paper; a new puzzle—maybe of the Alps mountains in Switzerland—for Aunt O. I loved wandering through the stores by myself with my own money, taking the bus to Corpus all by myself to do it, liked even having my money taken from me so I could get something I had selected for another, watching it being put in a container and zipped up to a cashier's window on a wire. And I always especially loved buying for my mother a perfume and powder called Heaven Sent in a blue box decorated with silver angels and stars.

Between Thanksgiving weekend when I shopped and the time a few weeks later—though it seemed much longer—when I wrapped the presents in white tissue (colored paper was scarce during the war) and for decoration stuck on blue and gold sticker stars and angels and tied them up with blue and gold ribbon and made—to compensate for the plain paper—enormous bows, I looked often at these treasures. We would go to Arkansas when school was out, would cut a real cedar tree from the woods.

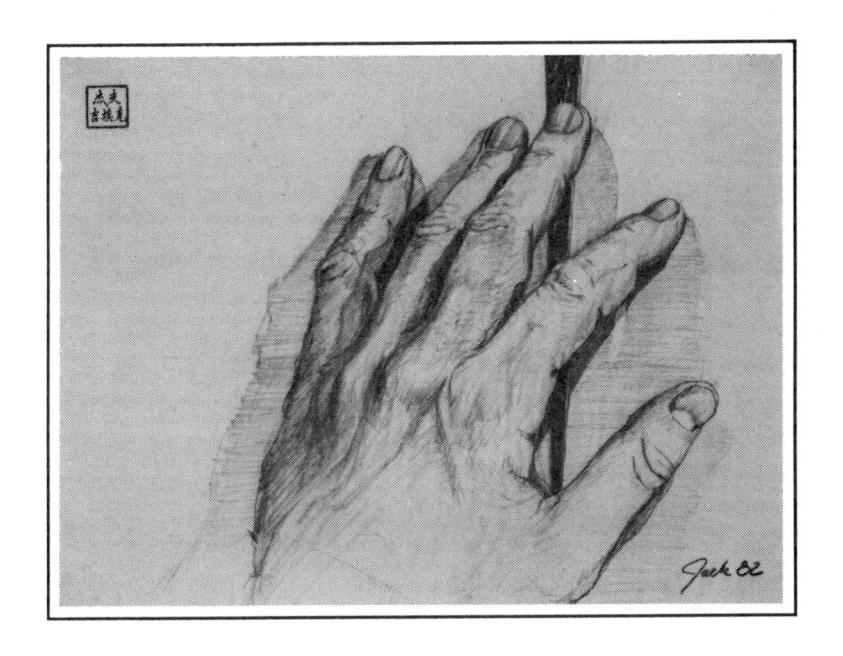

Wintershine

When we left for Christmas on the Hug the Coast, we seemed to climb. The land didn't actually begin to rise much until the Desota that Louise and Robby took turns driving left that highway and pushed into the pine trees the other side of Houston. If only because I was happy and when I looked at the map and saw we traveled North, the right direction it seemed to me then at Christmastime, all the journey seemed to me up.

My spirits, too, soared for I was returning to the place of my beginning and I looked forward to re-visiting the people and rooms and woods that I remembered. And to picking out the Christmas tree with my grandfather and later to stringing it with colored lights and bright ornaments as well as some that I made with crayons and construction paper, to hanging icicles on one at a time and to finally spinning the whole thing over with angel hair that pricked my fingers. And on Christmas morning to giving my carefully chosen and wrapped gifts to the family.

As much fun as I'd had in Texas shopping for those, paying for them with my savings and then choosing just the best stickers and ribbons for each one, I hadn't been in Arkansas long before I found something I wanted to give much more. I had heard my Uncle Lloyd and Aunt Jewel were separating. With new quarrels and separations in my family and with such uncertainty in the world, the men getting ready to go to war, I thought we needed special help this Christmas.

One day when I went walking in what my grandfather called "Wintershine"—for a mysterious shining lit up the frost and even the dead leaves that had fallen—I found in deep woods (far, far back from our property near the base of North Mountain) rocks of such unusual stripe and color that although I didn't pick them up when I first saw them, I knew I would finally have to collect and give them away.

Glittery gold streaks in some, turquoise in others, clear crystal in the quartz, they waited for me in the wildest and deepest part of the woods, way beyond Old Pete's place, beyond the Village of Men and the blackberry thicket where I had been lost one summer, were there the first day I had gone tramping, leaves from oaks and hickories crunching underfoot.

I had asked permission to hike right after breakfast and my mother consented on the condition that I dress warmly and watched where I was going, stuck to the paths and heeded my grandfather's warning about snakes under rocks. I promised not to turn any over and when I went out wore a heavy coat, mittens, long socks and a knit hat that covered my ears. Grandpa would have gone with me if he hadn't planned a day at the woodpile chopping and stacking wood, enough he hoped to keep the fireplace going day and night in the weeks to come.

When I went with Grandpa to Hot Springs Mountain in town, he always read me the sign that spoke of it being a National Forest and said that picking up rocks or cutting vegetation was unlawful. Although I had with my relations picked up pretty rocks many times and though these that I had just found weren't in the National Forest, they were of such quality that at first taking them didn't seem to me right. I would have to think about them I told myself and then come back if I thought making gifts of them for my family was the thing to do. Grandpa might use some in the birdbath he was building, Aunt O might like one in her kitchen window (how the crystal in the quartz would shine in that light!), Uncle Lyman could use them on his plans, my mother on her music, to weight the paper. I wouldn't tell I had found them. I would wait and if I thought picking them up was ok, take them when I came back.

The stones wouldn't be hard to find I told myself for they lay near the foot of a perfectly formed cedar tree, too perfect and too large to consider cutting, and near an unusually large bunch of mistletoe, such a lot that I broke off some pieces to take to Aunt O. When I was little I loved to pick holly and mistletoe up in the woods and didn't know until this moment that I could still find any. Aunt O had complained that mistletoe didn't grow in our woods anymore. She liked to hang it over her front door for luck and to get extra kisses from Uncle Lyman, and everybody, and to take some to Grandma's—Mother Merrill's as she said—on Christmas day to help decorate the dining table and to sweeten the atmosphere at the table. For some years there were, after too much strain and drink that reopened old grievances, bitter quarrels there. This year they were likely to be worse for now my Uncle Lloyd drank more than Uncle Lyman ever had and I was told for worse reasons. I heard my mother say Aunt Jewel had put him out of the house.

So many times I had heard Uncle Lloyd say that she was "like ice"— "Oh Jewel is a cold jewel"—that she wouldn't let him touch her and I heard Aunt O say that to touch her was most of what he had ever wanted to do, that he had worn himself out making money (and that was his gift), not for its own sake but to please her. They had been together since they were in their teens and took on a little wholesale business, beer and in the early days also cigars and candy, worked hard to keep it and had a grown son who spent too much and drank too much and now after all the years together they hardly spoke to each other although they were both coming for dinner on Christmas day. I thought if we hung enough mistletoe they would make up or at least not fight.

Yes, I decided I would give Aunt O the mistletoe, but I would keep the rest secret. Maybe after Christmas I would bring Grandpa or Uncle Lyman or Aunt O back to see the rocks if I decided not to give them or anyway to see the tree.

I thought on all this as I walked.

Then when I got back to the rooms in which we stayed I looked at all the places I thought the rocks would go when I brought them back; (I guess deep down I always knew I would bring them back, that for a while I had just wanted to contemplate the pleasure): Uncle Lyman's work table, Grandpa's half built bird bath, my mother's piano.

Wintershine, my grandfather always said, comes only when it's really murky and is meant in its peculiar fashion to put a glow on what has been too dark to define. When I set out again it was on a day like this. Except for the far light faintly glittering now and then onto the frosty leaves on the path and through the pines, the day was gloomier than usual and very cold. The women would never have let me set out if they had been at home instead of shopping in town.

That second time I went the way I always had, up Dread Hill, down one side of it to Old Pete's boundary and then past that and up again, past Pete's place and onto the red road that twisted its way through the woods to the Village of Men and past that, through the berry thicket and then to the left onto a little path that led into a thick wood at the base of the mountain, (North Mountain, the most elevated in our parts). When I looked up I noticed a pale bird flying in a ribbon of light, a large bird, from one of the far lakes maybe flying now in the direction of the river, that didn't want to get in the way of hunters. Was it just now making its way south for winter? Grandma said that until only a short time ago it had been warm.

Although I had come the same way on the same path I had used the first time, I didn't find the place of jeweled rocks and mistletoe. As I walked the day grew darker, the Wintershine as Grandpa called it, intermittent at first and then less and less frequent; my hands hurt with cold and my feet grew heavier and numb. Aunt O had told me to get more mistletoe. She said we would have a happy Christmas with so much kissing. Had a demon spirit removed what I wanted? Or had a quarrel in my own family stirred those spirits up and given them power to take over the woods? Was the place I was looking for somewhere behind me? Or still farther on?

I knew to find it I would have to depart the path by a little. But the place hadn't been hard to come upon before. I had taken this trail dozens of times since I was small and never had much trouble. The time I was separated from Aunt O when we were on a blackberry pick I had been lost in tangle but that day had been bright and hot and Old Pete whom I had feared, loathed even, had saved me and this day was cold with only a little light through the pine trees and that fading. Old Pete would be in his little house by a fire.

"Look down," I could hear Grandpa saying. "On a cold dark day if there's light nowhere else, the ground has it." (Too shy to look at Robby, our most dazzling family member, some of my first memories were of looking down, at the light that came from my own feet.)

Well, I had kept to the path, had looked down, and part of the way, the frost did sparkle. Had it also led me astray? Had I dreamed that clearing, the big, perfectly shaped tree, the glittering stones that might have washed down the mountain in a rain storm or tumbled down in a big wind? Why had I come on so dark a day? Had I dreamed the mistletoe?

I saw a clearing then. And although it didn't seem the right one, I walked into it and sat down on a stump. Yes, I told myself, I had gone through the berry thicket and instead of going straight up the narrow path to the top of North Mountain as I would on a hike with Grandpa to the pumice mine, I had turned to the left just slightly and taken a path and walked through a row of cedar trees just as I had a few days before, but this time I didn't see the big tree or white berries or shining stones. I must be in the wrong place. I wasn't sure I now knew my way back even so far as the berry thicket. I was losing confidence and becoming drowsy; I thought it must be below freezing. Every now and then I had to shake myself awake, numb as I was and half blind in the murky dark and cold. Should I just turn back? What was I going to do?

I saw then the big winged creature of refulgent light, very tall, twice as tall and more as the tallest tree, and just above or through it, a misty ladder that seemed at the same time to be a path, a stream of light that seemed to go into the sky and on and on (for just a moment I wanted to fly into it), a Being who had come for me, stood between me and all the rooms I had ever lived in and, now, all outdoors—the pure essence it seemed to me blown sky high of all shine. I lifted my freezing hands, heavy as stones, toward my face to block the nearly unbearable whiteness, though I thought I would probably have to be able to stand it, when with a flap of gigantic wings, whatever it was seemed to lift the trees, their roots dangling, and me with them blinking when it sat me down again— in just the time it took for me to shut my lids and open them to a world that was once again all murky gray—and was gone.

But this time I was in the right place, the mistletoe on one side of me, the cache of glittering rocks at my feet.

When I got home I didn't speak of the tree or my treasure, but sealed the rocks in boxes that I hid in the back of the guest room closet; on this visit the guest room was the one in which my grandparents insisted my mother and I stay.

But I did try to tell about the angel, if that was what I had seen.

I told my Aunt O when I first got back and saw her on the path and gave her more mistletoe. "Is that so, Pumpkin?" she asked in a casual manner, but not disbelieving.

I told my mother as she drew my bath water and rubbed my hands and arms and feet with hot oil, all the time exclaiming I might have frost bite. "Oh, baby," she said, "you are such a dreamer." But she and everyone else, even my grandmother, seemed truly glad to have me back. No one suggested switching me for having taken off. After considering what I told them I had seen, my mother and grandmother, too, said they expected I was just freezing and that I'd had a short dream in a light sleep. "You were so cold," they said together, "you went to sleep." And then added how lucky I'd been to be able to shake myself to.

Later after supper my mother let me open one of my Christmas presents early, flannel pajamas with feet in them (which I found inside the zippered back of a soft "Sleepy Time" doll) and as I sat in them by the fire I told my grandfather who listened seriously rather than just politely, listened not just to humor me or baby me, but because he cared about what I saw. "Sometimes," he said, "in winter when you need help in the woods the Wintershine grows. And gives it." He paused and then added, "Anyway, you got home safely by some good light."

Christmas was the coldest anyone could remember, but bleak (it didn't snow) and after his third eggnog early that morning Uncle Lloyd asked me to sing "White Christmas" and kept asking all day. "Annie, honey, sing 'White Christmas' for your sad old uncle." And though I did, I felt more embarrassed for us both than sad. Then late in the day when he saw me outside playing for a while on the rise of the hill near the old foundation (he was on his way to Uncle Lyman's and between houses) and had tears in his eyes and smelly breath even in cold, he stopped and asked again, "Sing White Christmas, Annie." I did feel bad for him then. What light we had was fast fading, the evening dismal.

But I was thankful that Uncle Lyman who now drank less and less was still all right.

And that he and Grandpa and my mother and Aunt O and even Robby and my grandmother had all liked the presents I brought back from the woods for them and the story I told about finding them. They had different versions about what really happened. I didn't know myself which was right. It should have been a happy Christmas, the dining table loaded down as it was—turkey and cranberries, oyster dressing and peas with little pearl onions—the doors all hung with mistletoe. If only there had been more kissing!

Everyone in the family was shy of touch except Aunt O.

Expectations on the night before had been hopeful. Everyone thought Jewel and Lloyd were patching things up. But when they arrived they barely spoke to one another—and there was always an icy silence between Jewel and my mother. Then as the day went on there was too much speculation about what presents cost and too much drinking and finally a quarrel broke out.

My Uncle Lloyd caught Jewel around the waist as she was passing through the dining portal and nuzzled her behind one ear. He had told her just minutes before how pretty she looked in the black wool dress with black mink at the collar he had bought her for Christmas; she wore the real diamond earrings he gave her for her birthday the month before. "Get away, Lloyd," she said, turning to push him from her. "You know how I feel about you." Her voice was, as always, soft. She barely spoke above a whisper, but we all heard, riveted, all of us at the table. "You are disgusting." He began to cry then and my grandmother, curling one side of her lip, yelled at him—as my mother and Robby eyed each other and Grandpa and Uncle Lyman looked at the floor (Aunt O was in the kitchen.)— "Straighten up."

By the time Aunt O came in carrying the platter of sweet potatoes in orange cups my mother had made, tiny marshmallows I liked so much on top, everyone was rigid and silent. Only the sound of Lloyd's sobbing penetrated the room. "Why, what is the matter?" Aunt O asked. "Will somebody please tell me?"

"Your brother-in-law," Jewel said quietly, "is drunk. Well, he'll have to stay the night here. After I have a piece of Mother Merrill's good pie" (a pecan) "I'm driving the Packard home."

And a few minutes later she did. As she drove down the hill my mother said, "Good riddance, Miss Bitch," and Robby laughed, and Aunt O sighed and said, "Oh, I don't know why we can't just have a nice day."

Later she and my mother and grandmother worked to the point of exhaustion washing dishes and putting food away and by late afternoon everyone was tired and cranky and let down and blue, grumbled and snapped at each other and at best dozed on beds and couches.

Although I had loved the mystery and formal beauty of the night before and early that morning giving my gifts and receiving some fine ones, too—my own illustrated Heidi and new skates and sketching pencils—I was disappointed in Christmas Day as I have been many times since. In the evening after I came in from playing and singing "White Christmas" for Uncle Lloyd I noticed the day had turned to sleet and I knew we would have a lot more days like this one without any presents or special food or mistletoe.

Still some moments had been good. Although Aunt Jewel rebuffed Uncle Lloyd under the white berries, Uncle Lyman who was shy had hugged everyone for a long time there and stayed sober all day. My grandmother said she would keep her rock, one with gold in it, on top of her sewing basket and my Uncle Robby told me he would carry his turquoise one for luck when he went off in the war. And those were the two people I thought might not like the presents from the spot I, with some help, found in the woods.

The tree that Grandpa and Uncle Lyman cut at the top of Dread Hill was a bushy pine, so green that we decided not to put icicles on it—only multi-colored balls and lights—or even to spin it over with much angel hair, just a light coating. After Grandpa and Uncle Lyman cut the tree, I spoke of the big cedar in the deep woods and Grandpa said I was right not to want to cut it, but to keep it growing there.

Christmas Eve the living room lit by only one floor lamp and my mother's piano light and the great fire from all the wood grandpa had cut, booming, we dressed every one of us in our best, mostly homemade, clothes; I in a short black taffeta my grandmother had sewn, a black taffeta bow in my hair (because I was fair the women put me in black a lot); Grandpa and my uncles wore their dark blue suits and elegant cream or wine colored ties, my mother a dark red crepe with shoulder pads which Grandma had also made, her hair pomped on top and in back pulled into a figure eight; my grandmother a bright blue real silk print with a lace collar, a perfect underpining for the broach I bought her; and Aunt O a wild black floor length dress with large white flowers, which she had ordered from a catalogue and which everyone said looked cheap and that she was too fat to wear. My mother played some classical pieces. Aunt O and my grandmother served fruit cake and cookies shaped like bells and trees and stars.

After the entertainment and refreshments were over and everyone retired and all but the tree lights were out, I came back in the darkened room just to sit for a long time and take it all in. I wanted to keep it and I knew I couldn't, except in my mind.

I didn't know how well I'd keep it. Is this what "keeping the Christmas" finally means?

Of what I had seen in the woods I remember the commentary almost more than what really happened there, just as I remember the newspaper account of my fifth birthday almost more than the actual party. My mother said I was rescued by my good sense of direction ("She always did have a good sense of direction."), my Uncle Lyman said by just plain "good sense," plus "a strong constitution," and my Aunt O chimed in, "and the imagination God gave her." My grandfather, of course, always insisted and I thought him closest to being right, for I knew whatever had done it was part of a natural order, that the elements in nature itself brought me home.

After that Christmas we spent another winter in Texas, a wild, wet one, for it rained nearly every day as if the elements had to weep for a world at war. And in the spring my mother had another of her glamorous piano recitals in the Community House on the stage, which my Uncle Robby decorated for the last time, where lumber yard workers from Cage's store placed double pianos and tubs of white and pink oleander and red hibiscus and other flowers picked literally by the truckload from neighborhood yards and fields around the countryside. In a long white net dress my grandmother had made, a gold cross my stepfather had sent from Alaska around my neck, my hair on top of my head in curls Robby had fashioned, I played three short, simple pieces and got through them all right although I felt that as the music teacher's daughter I should have done better. When my mother played at the end of the recital I wondered why I had even tried.

Except for another summer in Arkansas and another winter in Texas with Uncle Robby gone and Louise and I alone in the bare duplex with Bertha Oest on the other side—we were that winter without even a radio and some evenings I knocked on Bertha's door to ask if I could hear comedy or mystery shows—then still another summer in Arkansas, very hot with a trip to "A Thousand Drippings Spring" where we swam and saw the water snakes dozing on a far bank, the last I ever took with my grandfather, this was almost all of it, the childhood that plays over and over in my mind. But in memory one day with my grandfather stands out.

We went for a long hike through the woods and up North Mountain, to the top of it, past the pumice mine, took the whole day to do it. I had complained that I wasn't enjoying the summer, that it wasn't like those summers I remembered, that we didn't have any days in the woods hiking or berry picking anymore. Although I didn't understand this then, my grandfather was I expect too old to spend the time he had as a woodsman when I was a small child. Uncle Lyman was during this summer, his last before throat cancer and hospitalization, in Louisiana on a construction job, with Aunt O. As if touched by magic or a healing hand he was sober from the Christmas I have recounted. The Appleys' had moved to town just the month before, though Geraldine and Leona had long since married and gone, and the old house stood empty of all but its ghosts.

My grandmother had fixed us a good lunch of cheese sandwiches on homemade bread with carrot sticks wrapped in wax paper and fresh peaches off our trees and a thermos of lemonade. We took the familiar paths up Dread and then Old Pete's hill—Old Pete worked it even after we sold the property and everyone left for Texas—down the red road and into the berry thicket and then the trail that went to the top of North Mountain, all of it so hot and bright that I didn't then think of my trip to find my secret treasure in what Grandpa had called "Wintershine." So we didn't speak of that, but we did speak sometimes of dangers, snakes especially, and storms. In spite of the dazzling heat, a dark cloud—though it didn't seem threatening—hung over one side of the mountain and cast a huge shadow reminding me all at once of the giant Being of light I had once seen. Was this its other side?

We took the path straight up—and it was so steep that I had to hold on to one end of Grandpa's walking stick and he to the other, hard climbing that seemed to go on and on. And when we got to the top with all the countryside laid out before us for miles around—the finest view Grandpa said in the whole county—we stood, panting and wonder-struck before it. Then when we sat down and opened our lunch sacks and I unscrewed the top of the thermos to the lemonade, Grandpa told me how he had come as little more than a boy, just over twenty, with his young friend, sixteen, my grandmother who was also his bride, and stayed because he liked the look of the country and also knew it wanted building. He spoke then about how he had as time went on grieved for the troubles of his children more than for his own—Lloyd's pining for a woman who seemed to like things better than people, Lyman and my mother's frustrations that had come through hard times and not being able to fully use their gifts. But he said he was glad for what they had been able to do with them—my mother's students won scholarships and Uncle Lyman designed and constructed several really necessary bridges—and for what they were able to give me. As he talked, I saw it was raining in a far part of the landscape and that we would get none of it; it was where we were too hot and blue. "Grandpa," I said, "I will try to use mine for them." I meant of course my "gifts" though at the time I was none too clear on what those might be. I made up my mind to find out. He smiled and turned back to a surer subject. "You'll never see a more beautiful country." I thought I probably wouldn't, but I wanted to see them all. He put his arm around me then; the climb had worn him out he said and we decided to take our time going down.

Wintershine is published in a first edition of 1000 copies the first 400 of which are signed and numbered by the author.

BIOGRAPHICAL NOTE

Eve La Salle Caram is on the English faculty at California State University, Northridge, and has taught fiction writing in The Writers' Program at UCLA Extension for more than a decade. Born in Arkansas where she spent her early childhood, she grew up on the South Texas coast, attended the University of Texas, in Austin, received a degree in literature from Bard College, Annandale-on-Hudson, New York and studied fiction writing at Columbia University. She holds a Master's degree in English and writing from The University of Missouri, and taught fiction writing there and at Stephens College. She has published fiction, articles and poetry in numerous literary magazines including The Cottonwood, *The Greenfield Review*, *Snowy Egret* and *Sou'wester*. Ms. Caram is a member of PEN U.S.A. Center West and has three times been a Yaddo fellow. In 1991 Plain View Press published *Dear Corpus Christi*, her first novel.